Richard Wirick

ONE HUNDRED

SIBERIAN POSTCARDS

TELEGRAM

London   San Francisco

ISBN 10: 1-84659-015-9
ISBN 13: 978-1-84659-015-3

This edition published 2006 by Telegram Books

A full CIP record for this book is available from the British Library.
A full CIP record for this book is available from the Library of Congress.

Manufactured in Lebanon

TELEGRAM
26 Westbourne Grove, London W2 5RH
825 Page Street, Suite 203, Berkeley, California 94710
www.telegrambooks.com

This book is for Deborah

Моей Верной жене

And to the prompt and early-arriving
Maya and Evan

Ангелам

And finally, to the somewhat late-arriving
Amelia Paulina
around whose glad gift of herself
these strange tales subtend

Blossom, speed thee well

Acknowledgments

To the pros: Malu Halasa, agent extraordinaire, who knocks at the door (and, when she has to, kicks it in); my editors Mitch Albert and Rebecca O'Connor; André Gaspard, Mai Ghoussoub, Anna Wilson, Lara Frankena, and everyone at Saqi/Telegram.

To first readers: Deborah Bauman, Anthony Robinson, Kenneth Dekleva, Dean Ferguson, Victoria Pynchon, Mira-Lani Perlman, John Witte, Sandi Wisenberg, Jo Glanville, Claire Canning, Rose George, Peter Lyle, Samantha Gillison, Daniel Bourne, Jordan Davis, Nora Wong, David Katz, Paul Ruffin, Robert Phillips, Ekow Eshun, Masoud Golsorki, Carolyn Issa, George Garrett, Geoffrey Wolff, Whitney Pastorek and Shauna McKenna, Tim Page at *Tin House*.

To the slavists, anthropologists, linguists and Russophiles: Bruce Grant (NYU); Sara Pankenier (Stanford Dept. of Slavic Languages); June Leibovitz; Pieter Vibetowsky and his staff at the Scott Polar Research Institute at Cambridge; Anna Reid; library staff at London University's School of Slavonic and East European Studies; Svetlana Siliovicz, Martin Ruditsky, Chynira and Narina Rhamatova, Elvira Safiullina, Norrine Mtvhvhik, Gina Werfel.

To the editors of journals and magazines in which these *frissons* first appeared: *Another Chicago Magazine, Bakunin, Baltimore Review, Carolina Quarterly, CrossConnect, Dakota Quarterly, Faultline, Fiction, Folio, Indiana Review, Northwest Review, Quarterly West, Tank, Texas Review, Transformation.*

To my family: past, present, future.

'Reality,' of course, is man's most powerful illusion;
but while he attends to this world, it must outbalance
the total enigma of being in it at all.

Erik H. Erikson

Man can, without God, build a monument
out of the nothingness that crushes him.

André Malraux

Of course it's a tragic story, that's why it's so funny.

James Tate

1

Aviatrix

He stood watching the trails of jets, as he had done since he was a child. But in Siberia, it was especially important to know there were planes, even if you did not know where or when your next one was. So inconceivably vast were the distances – like those of Pacific or antipodal latitudes – that you had to know there was something powerful enough to get you from one world to the next. The sunset sky, the *vecher*, had grown the same violet as the plane trails. The great white and violet-turning mountain behind them, Goyen knew, was where the Aeroflot captain and his son had crashed an Airbus full of 340 people, bound from Moscow to Hong Kong. The pilot had let his fifteen-year-old boy take the stick in celebration of his birthday. There was no first officer in the cockpit. His father had dozed off. There are no corrections or redundancies to controls that have been neglected, even for a second. Goyen had once seen an Indonesian boy go forward into the right seat with his captain father, and had thought nothing of it at the time. But that was ten years or so before the crash here. Goyen wondered what everyone was thinking at the last minute, and looked up at the mountain. He remembered reading that it had been twilight.

2

Movable City

Centenario Italo Calvino

We were at a primitive airport in the Altai region. The man in back of me was returning to Mongolia and put a hard-shell suitcase, end up, on the conveyor belt as he presented his ticket. I was through already, holding my boarding pass, and the security woman motioned me over to her X-ray monitor. Dozens of little men were sawing timber inside the Samsonite, stripping, planing and loading the white spruce trunks onto trucks whose beds they tightened with tiny fiber cables. These roads of labor twined up through frilly garment pockets and zippered inner compartments. Signs divided them. There were tunnels, pulleys, elevators bringing in fresh crews and taking the exhausted ones away. Men took off their helmets and wiped their brows, and when they resumed their faces were contorted with microscopic grimaces of pain. At the top a foreman leaned out from the balcony of a shirt collar, surrounded by underlings with clipboards, giving directions with a stick no larger than a needle. The woman looked at the Mongol man. He smiled, and held up the forms on which he had truthfully checked the 'No' boxes for toxins, fruits and insects, liquid fuels, forbidden items.

3

Awe

Goyen's business partner had never been to Siberia before, and the crisp severity of the place pooled around him in his midnight stopover. This was the place, he knew, where trees exploded from the unbelievable temperatures, where the ice of the rivers thundered and pounded away at the pilings of city bridges. Standing on the tarmac in front of the Tupelov's engines, he marveled at the crunch of his step: the permafrost was buoyant, alive: as springy to the touch as the rubber asphalt he had run on as a teenage track competitor. When he exhaled, the cloud of his breath hardened and stood suspended for a moment, then fell crashing upon his boots like puffs of tossed-up sand. This was the 'breathing of the stars' he'd read of, and he tried it a couple of times before he heard the rising whine of whatever it was coming out of the mountains behind him. The man was running toward him out of the darkness; he was, after all, the only one who hadn't taken advantage of the warmth of the long, still-lit barge of the terminal lounge. The sound rose to a peal. He felt the waves of it sloshing over him like an undertow. When they washed him out of the rims of the turbine his severed hand had a single finger raised, a nubbin of wonder.

4

Loved a Woman
Who Wasn't Clean

Goyen had no idea the Hubshi woman would occupy his dreams, and even the half-sleep shreds of waking life that slowly soaked him every night into unconsciousness. He'd recognized her as a Khasbass: the Tatar cheekbones, a thin blue wire necklace hung with yellowed wolf teeth. She ran the canteen on the road he drove to the new Siberian geological site. He'd hung around one night after she closed and they flirted, listened to Moscow rap stations on the radio, drank grain alcohol and Armenian cognac. They'd groped each other standing up against the stockroom door. He touched the wiry region underneath her toolbelt. The first night she appeared as if inflated in front of his window, her face encrusted with pufferfishlike spines, the blue necklace trailing his furniture like a kite string. Subsequent evenings had her face assembling itself in internally collapsing and reappearing segments of silver, like an escalator of weightless, persistent mercury. He knew a shaman had observed their tryst. All visitors to these roads were seen as potential conquerors, contaminating agents. By the third appearance, she was insubstantial, foggy, filling the column of air before his bed like a drape of crystals. The window was slightly cracked and a breeze came in. She unfolded and dispersed, leaving a tang of kerosene and pine-scented gravel.

5

Hisses

Many of the Buryat myths involved snakes. They had a devastating, sometimes tragic role in the rearing of children, and the Soviet commissars often could do nothing until it was too late. Some of the parents practiced frontal applanation of their newborns' heads. The idea was to bestow a reptilian flatness and triangular general head shape, like that of most crawling serpents. They bound up the newborn's pliable skull with weights. They believed snakes were sacred, and that people with snake-shaped skulls would demonstrate enhanced intelligence and creativity. It had a positive, motivating, psychological force on the parents, and the children became freer, more vibrant, intuitive and original. We met a guide who told us he wished someone had had the imagination to do it to him when he was a newborn. He felt he would have gotten further in life, become a timber foreman perhaps, a Party member. He said he wouldn't have minded having a crenellated face, grossly distorted features. He moved the stuffed skull of a copperhead from one hand to the other as he talked.

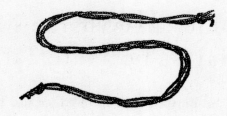

6

Come Live Inside Me, Said The Waterfall

The loggers of the River Ob lash logs together into rafts, like the ones you see in pictures in Mark Twain books. They build little pilots' sheds and wheelhouses, and sit on upturned boxes smoking cigars or corncob pipes stuffed with Don tobacco. They watch the waterfalls from passing tributaries for hours, mesmerizing, a wall of fiery magnetism filigreed with wisps of spray. After half a day of this, they shift their eyes to the riverbank, where the trees appear to rise. The doctors in Novosibirsk studied this phenomenon and offered the following explanation of the 'waterfall illusion': brain cells responsible for downward direction become weaker from prolonged stimulation, but cells responsible for upward motion do not, so to speak, become as tired, because they are not as stimulated. The illusion of upward motion results from the warring of two poles of neurons, with the upper pole winning out over the now-weaker downward pole. These upward motions of the trees were thought to be akin to shamans' visions, 'woods mirages'. The men thought they had eaten demon mushrooms, the visible world appearing to vanish like a rising playhouse curtain or a rocket lifting up and pulling away.

7

Hoods

The warmth of the body is kept from escaping by headwear. Without it, you are inviting the ghost to give you up in advance of death. The most common is fur-trimmed, though there is great variety even among these. They can be loose and floppy or tightened like watch caps, but they are the sole, sidelong aspect with which everyone presents themselves, the signature silhouette. Women, young and old, drape themselves completely in fur: there is no political correctness here with respect to the lives of animals. A Siberian Muslim will wear his fez-like stocking cap of darkling, brain-like lines and textures tipped jauntily forward, as if steering him back into the world. Teenagers give the hood an Eminem rapper take: gnomelike, tattered, torturously bound in headphone wires. Children look out from bright dozens of them, swarming around your knees on the Novosibirsk metro: sparkling, darting fish, looking for ways back into the crevices.

8

Iron Horse

Siberia owes much of its settled existence to the railroad. It was the main route in for both convicts and the scientific elite persuaded to live there in exchange for extra amenities, Party membership, tickets back to Moscow. From the plane window, different railheads bend down to cities like Tomsk and Novokuznetsk, but for the most part its aerial visual structure is one of a spidery, even crawl, west to east, across the muddy brown of the North Central Asian steppes. The oldest locomotives had elaborate snow sweepers, like American cow-catchers, with a widened inverted blade. Straw and chaff and flower petals from earlier time zones lay upon the boxcar tops as the train arrived in the cities. Once they found the skeleton of a Roma, a gypsy, wrapped in a canvas bag. Every farmer and merchant craved the wail of its whistle, because it was like the air coming into a sealed room. It was the very world. Whatever their sameness and monotony, the stops occupied the everyday conversations of the townspeople: the tram's punctuality, the condition of the cars, the way the crates and tightened bales came down the wooden loading draws with return addresses from unimaginable places: London, Reykjavik, Chicago. *Poezt, poezd,* the children said: the worm that winds its light of rescue. At night, its great cyclopean eye burned through the snowfall like a lantern mantle, like the heart-beams the icon Virgin pointed to inside her chest.

9

Speck–sized Screaming Heads

The Um-Sut Hotel in Abakan was where Goyen first heard them. The proprietor said this was what they were. They sounded like a faint choir to him as he lay on his bed with all of his clothes on, watching the ceiling. The size of pinheads, but with faces that were almost entirely mouth. Many holes of resoundingly singing receptacles. Roundish teeth, someone who had looked at them in a microscope said. Perhaps they themselves ate bacteria. Goyen imagined their voices going straight up in the air parallel with his eyesight, so clear and uncluttered was the sound, such dreadful full-throated hosannas. When he got up to walk to the bathroom his footsteps gave out a higher sound than the hum coming from the rest of the floor. Standing in the doorway waiting to return, he thought about taking a different path, a different series of steps. He waited for the sound of the toilet to quiet.

10

Loba

Wolves have the tiniest of pupils, black pricks that float in irises as blazing white as the snowfields that are their hunting grounds. Their paws are larger than a fox's or a dog's. In the sun the dark tips of their fur shines blue.

Their destinies have been mingled with that of all Siberians living in the last five centuries. To shoot one is to partake in its being as completely as the American Indians did with buffalo. You 'became the ghost' of the prey -- something deeper than transubstantiation or metempsychosis. When *otsi y deti* – fathers and sons – hunt wolves together they partake of something more substantial than tradition, a piece of the generational helix as binding as the patronymic surname. To stalk them is to pursue the last feature of the clan's identity. Pictures are always taken with the carcasses stretched out before the rows of dour men, kneeling, their shotguns broken open over their knees. At Yasnaya Polyana there are pictures of Tolstoy after a wolf hunt with his grandsons. The long limp pelts are stretched out on the drift they stand behind. It looks like God and His angels and archangels, assembled together in solemn excitement.

11

Persistent Animal

The beavers of the River Tom are chewing, chewing. Their teeth are larger than their paws or snouts, bristling with imperial ivory, and once the branches are snapped off the animals carry them forward in their mouths, great glittering bushes moving as if by themselves, like the Dunsinane trees in *Macbeth*. The muddy banks are filled with orbs of silent, walking bushes. Only when they reach the water do you see the mammal eyes, mercurial coals that gleam and then fade with the effect of pushing, the labour of swimming. They paddle for a moment and then float, the eye-lights flickering when the breeze stops blowing through. Whole sides of hills above the banks are stripped of leaves and twigs and the branches' knotted flowers, and paw and bough trails flare up lavender in the dying light. You cannot see them re-emerge, as they only surface inside the mounds they have built already. Once or twice the mounds stir. Until they are engorged with work again, their path is unremarkable. There is only a line going back to the shore, parting the water out of nowhere like an invisible knife. They shake when they crawl back onto the bank. Their teeth come out, the white little eyes look around.

12

Ursa

There were seven bears and only four people, so it wasn't much of a contest. The villagers were Ulan-Ude Buddhist Mongols whose ancestors had moved north from Ulan Bator to escape the Bolshevik violence there in the early part of the century, so they did not believe in weapons, not even machetes. They had a heraldic spear of some sort on the wall, but that was it. The bears had been wandering for some days and were very hungry. They surprised the family during the midday meal. The father had tried to rush at the first charging animal with a chair while his wife hid under a table with the children. The bear broke the father's back with a single blow of its paw. Once he was down, the others closed in and tore his limbs off before they began to feed. They smelled the mother and children under the table and tipped it over. For a moment, watching her husband being devoured, the mother had passed out. When she opened her eyes, one of the bears was pulling a child out from under her. When it was clear the bears had gotten each of her children, she simply gave herself over to them. The young ones were virtually swallowed whole, their bones nearly plastic as flesh. 'Like birds,' the rescue workers said to the reporter. They were standing in a great lawn filled with blood and pieces of the table. The journalist picked up a shred of the cloth that had covered it and held it over his nose.

13

Plague

The Siberian summer insects are pestilential. Mosquitoes grow large as hummingbirds, and hornets drift like sparrows from hive to hive. They are begotten, born and die like Yeats's beasts, their husks dropping into the rapids of the Ob to become a foaming blanket of confetti. Driving along its banks in a Jeep, a wasp will shoot into the side of your face and die, its stinger undeployed. Cars and passengers' faces run with blood and searching handkerchiefs. The headlights and grilles are caked with wings, antennae, giant eyes as black and slick as olives. But they are seen as the reverse of the biblical locusts, for many a prisoner or lost traveler has eaten the paste and juices of these creatures' bodies. They can be easily caught by hand, they are so heavy and slow. They lift up out of rotting trunks and hover, moving only inches at a time, as if gazing at their human captors. There is a Khasbass myth – a variation on the wicked stepmother theme – in which a baby is abducted by a runaway husband's mistress, who takes the form of a furry Luna Moth. Her wings are green blankets folded around the infant's neck; she cradles it under her as she glides on the *taiga* breeze, feeding it spruce bark and pine nut crumbs, the syrups of maples. When the mother finds the baby, she is sprinkled with green yarn, green flakes, green tufts of iridescent dust. In later life she becomes an acrobat, earthless and lithe, and the taint of the color can still be seen as she twists and unfolds her limbs between trapezes.

14

Status

It is the view of some Western Russians that Siberians are a backward and benighted people. Firstly, many are descendants of prisoners, as the region is to Western Russia as Australia and Tasmania were to England. Second, even though they grant intelligence and literacy to inlanders, knowing their numbers include an abundance of scientists, chemists and spies, they will still look for some failure of urban success in the Siberian, a view that he who has left had little left to lose and few other places to go. There is a view that the Siberian is avaricious and materialistic, that his hunger to transform the wilds must be modulated or it will internalize into a Hobbesian savagery. It is like the old saying that the Russian peasant 'would devour God himself'. To a Petersbuger, steeped in Europe, the Siberian is a cowboy, a frontiersman blind to God's embodiment in the uniform aesthetic of a *polis*. Muscovites look upon Siberians as a slowed-down, sleepy race, unable to maintain themselves in the stream of commerce that is the capital's boulevards. Rostovans, those wild unbridled people, wonder at the Siberians' quietude and decorum. To these Don residents, axe-shavers and carvers of wildwood phalluses, vodka consumers by the bucketful, remoteness has always been a convenient excuse for excess. Like the snow that covers Siberia, its critics look at it as unruffled, featureless, its overwhelming expanse an absence of the tertiary – pure oblivion. My driver in Kemerovo said her Moscow cousins will not visit her because she lives 'outside of the geography'.

15

Spirit Passage:
A Shaman Tale

Such is the process of the spirit entering its conqueror:

When a man kills another during a feud, he returns home and does not eat cooked food until the soul of the dead man approaches him. You can hear the dead man's soul coming because the spear which hangs from the stone head within the man drags on the ground and hits against the trees and bushes as he walks. When the spirit is very near, the killer can hear sounds coming from the dead man's wound ... He takes the spear, removes the spearhead and puts the spear end of the shaft between his own big toe and the toe next to it. The other end of the shaft is placed against his left shoulder ... The soul then enters the socket where the spear head was, and pushes its way upward into the leg of the killer, and finally into the body. It walks like an ant. It finally enters the stomach and shuts it up. The man feels sick, and his abdomen becomes feverish. He rubs his stomach and calls out the proper name of the man he has killed. This cures him and he becomes normal again, for the spirit leaves the stomach and enters the heart. When the spirit enters the heart it has the same effect as if the blood of the dead man had been given to the killer. It is as though the man, before he died, had given his life's blood to the man who was to kill him.

16

The Basement

What would a queen do here? The princess wife of Bakunin followed him into exile in the Siberian highlands in the 1840s and marveled at the 'receptiveness of nature'. She became a crusader for prison and clinic reform, bringing in doctors – including Chekhov – and getting them as far east as Sakhalin. Then she wrote a book about it. Exile was preferable to staying in the nerve center of terror that had created it.

A half a century later, the Romanovs were not as lucky, and there were many, many princesses among them. In Yekaterinburg, they were herded into a cellar for a supposed photograph. Bolshevik cavalry men with revolvers stood outside the room as they assembled, the prissy Nicholas duped and suckered into lending a hand, adjusting his children's positions. At the sergeant's orders, a captain entered and read the Bolshevik 'sentence' written by the Duma the night before. When he heard the word 'death', *smert,* Nicholas said 'No!' and raised his hands, which were in turn greeted with the row of raised Colts from across the room. The shooting went on for twenty minutes, bullets ricocheting everywhere, bouncing off the children's pearl buttons and the older daughters' hidden jewels, finally making bone chips fly from the skulls of the fallen who still groaned or moved. All the Romanov aversion and escapism, all its feckless beauty, ended here. Privates and drivers piled the bodies onto a wagon and drove it miles away. They were thrown into a pit and burned with gasoline. From under the cloak of his tripod, the cameraman had lifted a Markov pistol, but never fired.

17

Ovid in Siberia

Transformation is in abundance in a Georgian tale that moved eastward to the frontier after the Revolution. It is called 'The Master and His Apprentice'. The Devil takes a boy as an apprentice and teaches him magic. The Devil wants to keep him there but the boy tries to escape again and again, and each time he is caught he grows more and more despondent. He practices his magic in the dark stable that is his cell.

A column of sunlight comes into the stable. The boy traces the crack in the door from which it came. He changes himself into a mouse and runs out through the crack. The Master changes himself into a cat, which chases after the mouse.

The transformations proceed at a frenzied pace. Just as the cat opens its mouth around the mouse, the mouse turns into a fish and jumps into a nearby stream. The Master turns into a net and swims after the fish, which turns into a pheasant just as it is being lifted out of the water. The Master becomes a falcon, and just as it closes its talons on the brown and green fluff the pheasant becomes a bright apple, dropping from its stem onto the lap of a king. The Master becomes a knife in the king's hands, and as the flash of the knife comes down the apple disintegrates into a trail of millet. The Master changes into a hen and pecks each of the grains except one. That one grain becomes a needle, and the hen and her chicks become a thread that filters through its eye. The needle bursts into flame and the thread is incinerated, falling into a thin line of ash. This is the Master's corpse, this long filament of cinders. The needle takes the form of the boy again, who returns home to his father.

The message of linear transformation and escape seems to be: persist, change location rapidly, persevere. The change, the change necessary for salvation or rescue, will come into you if you perform these tasks. It will come into you almost effortlessly, in the manner of an occupying spirit. There is a light ahead, and ahead of the light you are free.

18

The Blizzard Voices

The Sakhat family hadn't made it out of the wagon and into the *yurt*. It was the storm of 1888, and skeletons were still being dug up from the bog three years later. The wind had blown the blinders off the Sakhat horses, Mongolian stallions which might otherwise have plowed forward undaunted. The wind blew an entire drift, some thirty feet high, over the children, and the father went back for them, though he had broken free of the wind and was only two hundred feet from the shelter's door. The mother stayed at the sleigh door, just having stepped out and called for her children to come back. She thought the drift would pass them by entirely and leave them struggling, upside down like flipped bugs perhaps, but still beating the odds, getting the generous second chances of children and emerging alive. She was found buried to the neck in ice.

Her tongue was frozen to her metal teeth. Stones and brush had gathered around her head, and her hair came away in handfuls of matted, crystalled nettles.

19

The Bird Church

At first it is a peep, twitters, a solitary pair of notes unjoined to companions, sweet shrill, sweet shrill, sweet shrill in counterpart. This is the canopy adjusting itself, before taking on a form. There is no design, of nature or man or otherwise, in this incipience.

These sounds are not yet audible to the human ear. They are *in* themselves, the spirit in itself, not yet come down to the place of being for itself and others. These are the sparrows coming, the fixtures of summer. They are the first spilling over, the seepage of the divine down to the visible, mutable earth. Their voices are as indistinguishable as mesh, but as much a presence, as clear and complete a covering. It is the piping of ancient women's voices in caves, the infinitesimal fluting of hummingbird-like rings of sibyls. It seeps into the air as softly as the air's own change of color. Dawn or twilight, the voices are the high, high engines of the turning day. Their lower notes are at the highest register of human hearing. The leaves rise up and flutter at their sound, parched things leaning to a kind of rain.

Then come the tenors, the wood sounds of thrushes and starlings. It is an echoing, a rising and falling into itself, sea-like, incessant. Wood and air, one blowing through the other. The notes rise and fall as the wings and legs flap from the sagging branches. This is the greatest of ululations, rising crescendos of sound that layer and pull and flatten and even out, but fit perfectly into one another – notched and puzzle-cut, settling into place with the breeze's push.

The basses are the last, the deep male sound. These are the sea-bottom lantern fish of birds, the pulses of animal skins and tympanis. These are turkeys and grouse and quail. Their voices blurt from baggy flaps of skin, from paunches and tumorous aprons swelling and sagging like bellows. Spirit has come back to the earth in them. They will never fly or rise. This is their home. Why would they leave?

20

Imagined Ancestors

Many Siberians were royalists in the eighteenth century, and many used any excuse to trace their lineage to the Romanovs. A local town official showed me a biscuit-tin painting of Peter the Great and his family. The colors were garish. The shapes of the sitters' features and hair had a vivid, avuncular freakishness. Peter, of course, was hideously tall, his stature bordering on that of a giant. The Empress had a hook nose and frown, with skin as gray as Neva water. The nervous, feckless son – neither I nor the ombudsman could remember his name – showed all the marks of his destiny: demons of inbreeding, whippings at the admiralty boarding school, death at his father's hands. The others were indistinguishable, blending into one another like a basket of pastries. The king's and queen's eyes held all the fabled, expected thirst for butchery, for building monuments on their peoples' bones. *Can there be,* the hands – my guest's, which passed before the picture – seemed to say, *no greatness without cruelty?*

21

The Cossacks

It was the ordeals they had gone through that had torn this strange manifestation of vigor out of the breast of the Russian people. The erstwhile towns and princely domains, with their feuding and trading, had disappeared and their place had been taken by warlike settlements linked through common danger and hatred of the heathen predators. The unbreakable resistance of this people saved Europe from the merciless hordes to the East. The Polish kings had replaced the petty princes and become the official, though weak and distant, rulers of these vast lands. They had realized early on the advantage of having the plains inhabited by a warlike, free-roving race, and tried to encourage and preserve the Cossacks' wild way of life. Under their remote guidance, the Cossacks elected headmen and divided the territory into military districts.

They had no visible, regular army but, when a war or an uprising broke out, each man rode in, fully equipped, to report and receive his gold piece from the king. Within a week's time a force assembled which could never have been recruited. When the emergency was over, the trooper went back to his field or river, traded, brewed beer – in a word, became once more a free warrior.

'Who can tell? We are scattered over the entire steppe, and wherever there's a hillock, there's a Cossack.'

22

Prometheus

By the middle of the nineteenth century, explosions – man-made and fuelled by gunpowder – had become the new sorcerer's fire. Anarchists once again spread their counsel from the White Sea to the eastern steppes. Nechayev was chief among them, and the model for the protagonist in Dostoevsky's *The Devils*. His 'Catechism of the Revolutionary' is filled with the hiss of fuses, with conflagrations, explosions, pops and bangs. For all their contempt for the religious and their exaltation of reason, the Anarchists described their weaponry in mystical speech. Their arms would rise up as if by themselves from the peoples' animal indignation and need. The bomb that killed a vice-Tsar in his carriage was said to have been thrown so that 'it skipped in the air, as if a magic bird or animal'. This first 'smart' bomb's honing circuitry was the product of a wizard's energies. It hurt no one in the crowd. People doubted it could have been launched by human hands.

23

Holy Men

The West and Central Russian holy men were called *khlysty*, a sect devoted to the transformation of the soul by way of the mortification of the body. They stood for hours in swamps on the steppe, placing themselves at the mercy of mosquitoes and midges, never eating meat, which they believed 'blackened man, just as fish would whiten him'. Their brethren claimed that each possessed an imperceptible halo, and their eyes burned with a liquid, iridescent light, their gleam becoming at times almost unbearable.

In the waning days of the Empire, Rasputin would answer the Czarina's questions by causing teacups to move and making napkins fold and unfold themselves. The court and the royal homes became his troubled, mesmerizing stage. The mazes of his questions were said by his detractors to 'contain the ghosts of language' and to answer themselves. They reduced all inquisitors to silence and fear. His upraised hand was like a gnomon, the shaft of a sundial harkening the end of an age.

24

Ouija

The *khlysty* had the power of prediction down to the *n*th degree. Rasputin predicted the assassination of Prime Minister Stolypin by seven days; it was, like Lincoln's, a head shot in a theater, after an impossible series of police blunders. The Extraordinary Commission now took a special interest in the rumors that Rasputin was somehow linked to Stolypin's death. He was under constant surveillance. The faithful remained rapturous of his accuracy; the suspicious made sure he was trailed by guns.

The *khlysty* and their followers came under relentless attack after Stolypin's death. The writers Artsybasher and Kamensky spread stories of the Siberian monk hordes' 'orgiastic rejoicing' and 'mass group sinning'. But for every step forward in the battle against them, the Russian thirst for transcendence and unexplainable healing gave the practitioners extra stabs at public relations. One of the Czarina's friends, Lilli, had a son fall deathly ill. A *khlyst* was brought in, bent over the dying child and shook him, piercing his sleeping forehead with the now-famous icy stare. The mother was about to stop him, fearing her son would be frightened to wake to such a strange face. The boy opened his eyes and reached out toward the peasant's tangled, ratty beard, whispering, 'Uncle, Uncle. By Christ, you have come.'

25

Dionysis

Sexuality was as much as part of the Siberian mystic's trade as sacred books or chants or spells. None of these men were celibate – all were prodigious, mightily virile. Their powers were said to make their sperm good swimmers. The science of hexes was most efficient in its own multiplication. Rasputin had the ultimate come-on line to the ladies of Alexandra's court: sexual intercourse with me, the argument went, was the most direct form of communication with God. It was 'quicker even than prayer'.

26

The Babel Face

If the poet must 'wear all the masks' the short story writer, Isaac Babel, did Yeats's concept one better. His visage was a protean, amorphous thing, from accounts of witnesses. Here is Paustovsky coping with the difficulty:

I'd never met a person who looked less like a writer than Babel. Stocky, almost no neck ... a wrinkled forehead, an oily twinkle in the small eyes; he did not arouse any interest. He would be taken for a salesman or a broker. But of course this was true only if he did not open his mouth ... Many people could not look into Babel's eyes. He was by nature an 'unmasker', he liked to put people into impossible positions and he had the reputation of being a difficult person. Then Babel took off his glasses, and his face became at once helpless and good.

27

Abundance

What goes east from the port to Sibirsk ends up in the high, grass-bordered kiosks, the fragile little card stacks of the far steppe villages. Wines from Bessarabia, Haifa oranges, pickles in rum, flaxen scarves, sparkling jars of claws and hooves and heads (of fish, grouse, boars). And everywhere, in every form – fresh or dried and splintered into hardened, blackened stars – the mushrooms that for Russians are the coarsest, most insistent form of hunger's love: what housemaids call 'dogpeckers', cocks of the stirring, waking ground.

28

Abundance II

Descriptions of mountain flowers at the beginning of Tolstoy's *Hadji Murad*:

Red, white, and pink scented tufty clover, milk-white, ox-eye daisies with their bright yellow centers and pleasant spicy smell; yellow, honey-scented rope blossoms; tall canapules with white and lilac bells, tulip-shaped and surrounded with vetch; yellow, red and pink plantains with faintly-scented, neatly arranged purple, slightly pink-tinged blossoms; cornflowers, bright blue in the sunshine and while still young but growing paler and redder towards evening or when growing old; the delicate, quickly withering, almond-scented dodder flowers.

29

Black Sea Jerusalem

The Jews of Odessa were, to some degree, free to take part in the general life of the city. They were, to be sure, barred from schools and from numerous businesses, and sufficiently isolated when *pogroms* swept the city. Yet all classes of the Jewish community seem to have been marked by a singular robustness and vitality, by a sense of the world, and of themselves in the world. The upper classes lived in affluence, sometimes in luxury, and it was possible for them to make their way to a Gentile society in which prejudice had been attenuated by cosmopolitanism. The intellectual life was of a particular energy, producing writers, scholars and journalists of very notable gifts; it is in Odessa that modern Hebrew poetry traces its rise with Bialyle and Tchemichovsky. As for the lower classes, Babel represents them as living freely and heartily. In their ghetto, the Moldovanka, they are more contained by economic circumstances than religious ties. They were massively engaged with the world, of a Brueghel-like bulk and brawn; they had large, coarse, elaborate nicknames; they were gangsters made by Babel into Robin Hoods, 'good bandits' of the Black Sea's massive capital.

30

Return to the
Hotel Kuzbass

Once again the cloudless, crisp blue sky, but this time filled with the sun that so withholds its love from these northern lands. It rose out of the dry, brown kindling of the *taiga* orchard, like a gas jet waiting to explode within a mound of sticks. Hours ago before dawn, the wind had carried our voices and footprints away as we dismounted the plane and crunched toward the transport buses. Now the afternoon is as mild as Northern California's, and the ice on our window ledge is beginning to melt. Men mill in the hotel parking lot, unpicked for day labor in the timber camps. They squint and look upward, twisting off the caps of half-liter vodka bottles. By three, it is so hot I cannot sleep. My wife is preparing papooses and slings for our four-hour drive to the orphanage. Extreme to extreme. From starless black to an orange sun, to the final pink of the newborn's hand. Ice slides away and drops off the window ledge. The men look up.

31

Tyger, Tyger

There is terrain here that is completely independent of the *taiga* and the tundra of the steppe. It is a monsoon forest found nowhere else in Russia, filled with wildlife from the northern *taiga* but also from China, Korea and the Himalayas. The woodland floor of Ussuriland is lush, the heavy branches thick with lianas, vines, the nests and coves of canopy animals.

There are brown and Asian black bears, sables and wolves. But Siberia's own tiger, the *amur*, has given this place its new name and symbol. Its fur is silver-white rather than the usual orange, and it is larger than any tiger, the largest sub-species of the cat family. The native Nanai ('Nanaytsy' in Russian) worshipped them. Nanaytsy left a token wounded sow behind after every boar hunt, as this was the tiger's favorite prey. Sufficiently hungry, the tigers will kill livestock, humans, groups of humans. *Amur* means 'old man' in the Nanai language. Fathers counted out the sightings of these lordliest of creatures on the palms of their sons, saying, 'Grandfather, Grandfather'.

32

Trust

A legend from west of here, in Kislovodsk, tells of a girl from a rich family who falls in love with a boy from a poor one. Her father won't let her marry her true love, as the old man had promised her to an old and ugly but rich merchant. She refuses the match and runs away with the boy, her family pursuing them to the edge of a cliff outside of Kravedchesky. As they stand on the cliff's edge, the boy looks her in the eye and makes her promise to end their lives then and there, foreclosing her dull future as a merchant's wife. The girl agrees, but says she is afraid. She suggests he jump first. He falls the four hundred feet of the cliff's full height, crumpling like a flower on the rocks below. Looking down at his splattered body, the girl decides against it. Her parents run to the cliff's edge and surround her. She marries the merchant the following spring. His grown children regard her warily at the wedding, circling the outer limits of the banquet tables.

33

Wolf-hunting: Summer

From Tolstoy's *Childhood*:

The whole field swarmed with sheaves and peasants. Here and there among the tall thick rye where the sickle had passed could be seen the bent back of a woman reaping, the swing of the ears as she grasped the stalks between her fingers, a woman in the shade bending over a cradle, and scattered sheaves upon the stubble which was dotted all over with cornflowers. In another quarter were peasants clad only in their shirts, without their tunics, standing on carts loading their sheaves and raising dust in the dry scorched field. The village elder, in boots and with a coat thrown over his shoulder and tally-sticks in his hand, seeing papa in the distance, took off his lamb's wool felt hat, wiped his ginger hair and beard with a towel, and bawled at the woman ... Two *borzois* with their tails curved tautly in the shape of a sickle, and lifting their feet high, leaped gracefully over the tall stubble, behind the horse's heels. Milka was always in the front, with her head down seeking for the scent. The chatter of the peasants, the tramp of the horse and the creaking of the carts, the merry whistle of quail, the hum of insects hovering in the air in motionless swarms, the smell of wormwood, straw and horse's sweat, the thousand different lights and shadows with which the burning sun flooded the light yellow stubble, the dark blue of the distant forest, and the pale lilac of the clouds, the white gossamer thread which floated in the air or lay stretched across the stubble – all these things I saw, heard and felt.

34

Euphony

Abakan, Amur, Amgun, Alma-Ata, Bodunov, Buryat, Domodedovo, Kazan, Kuznetsk, Khabarovsk, Lermontov, Muzhna, Magadan, Novgorod, Oryl, Peredelkino, Rostov, Samarkand, Siberskat, Tuymen, Taganrog, Uzbek, Ulan-Ude, Volgograd, Voznesensky, Yakutsk, Yerevan, Zhukova, Zima, Zima, Zima, Zima.

35

Rider By My Side

You know the economy is going downhill when everyone in the country becomes a gypsy cab driver. With the exception of the mafia's Bentleys, which fly by with their blue, carte-blanche police lights throbbing, almost any car will stop when you lift your hand. You won't just find teachers and college students at the wheel but salesmen, merchants, low-level executives and housewives with babies squinched down in tight belted car seats.

When my friend the diplomat took me to the bottom of Embassy Hill and raised his arm at the corner of the Ring Road, I thought it was a normal taxi he was seeking. He didn't explain.

Most of the people who stopped in the two weeks I was visiting him were teenagers. We'd be going to his home in the diplomatic enclave of Rosynka, in far Northwest

Moscow, and the kid would usually bargain hard for that kind of distance. Given the nightmare of its traffic and the tax-starved, cratered roads, almost any ride in Moscow started with a fifty-dollar demand. Rosynka was an odyssey, through outer ellipses of congested 'feeding' roads and threads of two-lane blacktop knitting the birch forests. The kid would usually hold firm at seventy dollars, but Kenneth could get him down to around fifty with a small gas tip thrown in. Often, when Ken saw the driver giving way, he, too, with grace, would give way. It brought back to me, after years of being away from Latin America, the whole *kung fu* of bargaining, winning by seeming to yield.

The driver we got on this particular day was neatly turned out, with Euro-lizard black-framed glasses and terrible, open, bleeding acne. His Lada was passable, above average. Ken again did the bargaining and we got in the cramped back seat, an empty gas can between our feet.

Out where the last of the rings hit the northwest highway, in the longest, emptiest stretches of unlit, bermless waste, the Lada began to sputter. It surged at points so the accelerator felt stuck to the floor, but after six or eight pathetic dieselings the engine gave out completely and the car came to a stop in the right lane. There was enough of a straightaway behind us that people could see us from a great distance. No surprises. But the speed of passing cars was terrifying, shaking us where we sat, with the driver tinkering up under the hood raised on its fragile rod.

Ken got out and then I did, fearful of somebody clipping us or stalling themselves into our ever-widening repair area: tools, rags, bottles, boxes with layered trays, more cans but none with gas in them.

Finally, another car pulled over in front of us. The driver got out and brought half a gas can over to us. Our driver took it, paying with the tip we'd given him in advance, and then emptied the fuel into one of his own hollow canisters. The Russian passing between them was too rapid even for Ken to follow, but ended up with our man indicating that more than fuel was at issue, and that we should go with the new prospect. We gave our stranded driver a twenty and a ten, and he seemed satisfied.

From the back of the new vehicle, we watched the first driver approach his car, which he'd started up again for some reason. From forty or fifty yards away, our car spitting up gravel, we watched him pouring the gas in. After another hundred yards we were once again in the flow of metal, too late to do anything, and we saw flames burst up around the front of his car and leap onto his arms.

36

The Given and the Made

I went to a Chechen junkyard on the outskirts today to get a carburetor for the diplomat's Lada. The Chechen underworld controls all the used auto-parts markets in Moscow and, some claim, in the entire Russian Federation. After the theater hostage incident in Moscow in 2000, then after the Beslan school massacre in North Ossetia in 2004, the Caucasus natives are a people treated with an almost implacable hatred by many white Russians. As liberal as a group of the latter may appear, the assassination of however compromising a Caucasus Islamic leader is seen always as a victory, an erasure of vermin. I ran into one in his newspaper offices recently. Bedayev was on the run and the two 'black widows' had blown up a pair of planes flying out of Domodedovo, and there had been other suicide bombings. The journalist fancied himself a historian of ideas and had been reading a lot of Erik Erikson. He gave the following account of things, which I offer with no opinion:

The Caucasus Muslims have no nation, or only the most teetering of individual states, states being defined in Hobbesian terms as entities with a degree of infrastructure and a monopoly on the means of violence. Accordingly, the minds of these warriors are consumed with dueling concepts: battles between totalisms or absolutes that one could never imagine in Saudi Arabia or Iran, where the state puts its full force behind the absolute of sexual shame and hiddenness, the negation of sensual pleasure.

In contrast, Caucasus Muslims display all the forces of the sacred and profane *in balance*. The earthly and the pious mix with dazzling attractiveness, and this allure seems to grow the more these people are oppressed. It is what attracted Tolstoy to them, when he was defending against their raids as a young army officer in the 1860s.

Like the ideal human balance envisioned by Martin Luther, the Chechen Muslim encompasses both kinds of 'total states' in the mixture of his personality. The fighter for Allah here is both a total sinner (gambling, smuggling) but, as long as the mission is *jihad*, always blessed as well as damned, both alive and dead. As Erikson said of Lutherans, the Chechen Muslim cannot strive 'by hook or by crook, to get from one absolute state to another;

[he] can only use his God-given organs of awareness in the here and now to encompass the paradoxes of the human condition'.

So the Chechen soldier must accept at the same time his ruffian, outlaw urges and his piety to Allah. Only by holding them in balance can he confirm his identity. What appears to the outsider as religious submission is really mastery of fate; what appears as banditry is actually a weapon against the infidel. There is tremendous free will here – the warrior is the blender, the shaper of his urges, and he can take both enjoyment and a sense of usefulness from them.

When the soldier turns to suicide as a method of battle, he appears to have lost this balance of opposites. The drives that the conscience holds in check overwhelm that conscience. He surrenders to a spirit of non-existence and self-destruction that is simply another biological urge, one of the urges the ego considers as beneath and outside itself at the same time it is mesmerized by them. Suicide as a weapon can be called for by a ruler or commander, but to the true soldier *intentional* self-destruction is futile. No soldier is effective dead, no matter how many of the enemy he takes with him.

To the true soldier, the balancer and shaper, the suicide entreaty should be as repugnant as any of the other unchecked biological instincts. It is just another unbridled portion of what Freud called the *id*, but one far graver than sexual urges or a sense of public recklessness. It is the death instinct, the *spiritus moribund*, boiled down into a single person, a single event, a single travesty. Missions can be advanced by self-sacrifice, but not self-destruction. Suicide is altruism blotting out the self entirely, the mass man occluding the man. (Again, soldiers focus on the here and now: *that* is their spiritual advent, not some notion of Paradise.)

Mindless, commander-ordered battle suicide is a sort of id-intoxication, a poisoning. The self lets the reins drop and lies down on the back of the id-monster's fury. This is not soldierly. It is most certainly not Chechen. Control of what would otherwise be wild has always been the Caucasian hill peoples' watchword. Their power over horses and other beasts of burden was always their very symbol as a people. No Caucasus image or sketch exists in Tolstoy without the horseman and his almost mystical power over the animal. With that came mystical power over all other aspects of life, its preservation in the face of overwhelming odds. The Caucasus warrior 'looks life in the eye, looks the weather and the mountains in the eye', as Tolstoy wrote in *Hadji Murad*. He does not give himself over to them. He does not own them, but they are his companions.

One thinks of the captured Chechens in the longer Tolstoy stories, how their features and qualities draw their jailers in with a hypnotic effect. The prisoner does not sink into misery. He is defiant, his fists on his hips. His features – especially his eyes – could be large and prominent or small and hidden; the eyes are deep, unfathomable. They were never glazed with the sheen of annihilation. The Chechen always fought back. If captured and marked for death, he wouldn't be satisfied with the soldier's usual insistence on a firing squad over hanging. He would fight as they came for him. He would take one of his captors out in the process. He was a hawk, terrible and swift as lightning among the rest of humanity, which rested ledges and ledges below him, mere sparrows.'

37

States of Matter

Always the cloudless violet sky of the back country: from the Urals to the Mongolian border, the firmament seems a long, clear swath of blazing nothingness. Around you on a walk, the pale green, prickly foliage of the raspberry canes tangled with weeds. Nettles with slender flowering tops stretch up, and fat-leaved burdocks with blue-pink blossoms the same color as the dawn or twilight sky, so the green seems to bloom into any empty space, like the blown away manes of dried-up dandelions. Each new growth crowds out the old, forces it down into damp black compost. All that rises feeds on all that dies. There is no traffic on the road, but out on the horizon, in the hillocks around Kemerovo, smokestacks chug their breath into the still, unchanging morning.

38

Banya

The Siberian *banya* was more a center of the household than elsewhere in Russia, and its rituals of steam and cedar accommodated pagan and Christian doctrines alike. It was medicinal, the 'people's first doctor' (vodka was the second, raw garlic the third). The folkloric and magical beliefs associated with it are too numerous to mention. Life could literally begin in the bathhouse, as it was a place for giving birth. The mother was purified of the blood-birth and placenta there. Given the Orthodox associations of Christ's bloodless birth, she could be wiped free of all physical traits of fallen womanhood. Bride and groom went to (separate) bathhouses the night before the wedding. These were pagan bathing rites that came from the time of the Otskoi and Tatar shamans, but joined easily with the Christian Epiphany and Shrovetide ('Clean Monday') ablutions surrounding *Paskalni*, both new and old calendar Easters.

39

One Note

In the Siberian count's serf orchestra, each peasant was given a primitive instrument: a pipe, a recorder, a two-string lute or *balalaika*, a *gusli*. Each learned a single note, a unique placing of their fingers, and nothing else. There were so many musicians that significant sections of symphonic movements could be played, so easily could the abundance of players accommodate the requirements of the music's timing. The maestros were inevitably Finnish or French. When the baton was raised, each player was poised to carry through the act that reflected his entire life – singularity of service to a whole, a class or family, with no one part aware of the role of any other. Each of them were like blind stars, blinking without thought into trails.

40

Wind of the Wing of Madness Passed my Face

First accounts of depressive madness by Tolstoy, in diary form (Siberians called it becoming 'woods queer'):

The journey was a pleasant one for me. My servant, a young, good-natured fellow, was in just as good spirits as I. We saw new places and met new people and enjoyed ourselves. To reach our destination, we had to go about a hundred and forty miles, and decided to go without stopping except to change horses. Night came and we still went on. We grew drowsy. I fell asleep but suddenly awoke feeling that there was something terrifying. As often happens, I woke up thoroughly alert and feeling as if sleep had gone forever. 'Why am I going? Where am I going to?' I suddenly asked myself. It was not that

I did not like the idea of buying an estate cheaply, but it suddenly occurred to me that there was no need for me to travel all that distance, that I should die here in this strange place, and I was filled with dread. Sergey, my servant, woke up, and I availed myself of the opportunity to talk to him. I spoke about that part of the country, he replied and joked, but I felt depressed ... Everything seemed pleasant and amazing to him while it nauseated me.

−1888

41

Childhood

The bond between child and caregiver, and between children and caregivers' children. The daily *fait aplomb* with those the infant sees every moment of the day, the parents absent, the serf-nurses filling the void of motherhood. The everydayness of needs being met, the ability of an immediate, reasonable presence to satisfy it. The ability of my daughter, never having heard a man's voice in eight months of life at an orphanage, to accept my unanalyzable, repetitive *thereness*. Herzen, from *My Past and Thoughts*:

The resemblance between servants and children accounts for their mutual attraction. Children hate the aristocratic ideas of their grown-ups and their benevolently condescending manners, because they are clever and understand that in the eyes of grown-up people, they are children, while in the eyes of servants, they are people. Consequently, they are much fonder of playing cards or lotto with the maids than with visitors.

Visitors play for the children's benefit with condescension. They give way to them, tease them, and stop playing whenever they feel like it; the maids, as a rule, play as much for their own sakes as for the children's; and that gives the game interest. Servants are extremely devoted to children, and this is not the devotion of a slave, but the mutual affection of the weak and the simple.

42

Books of Number

In far south Tuva, or Tuvalu, lived the Kara-Khaaks, or Kara-Khem. Anthropologists from Berkeley, Kroeber's acolytes, had come in the early part of the century and run an ethnographic study of these people out of the university in Kyzyl.

The Kara-Khaaks presented a fascinating picture of how number and quantity came to be a settled fixture of civilized life, something that really hadn't happened, in any culture, until about the seventeenth century. As a result of the natives' extreme isolation, these two mathematical-spatial notions were almost entirely bound up with body-based counting systems, and with quantity as a function of ground space, i.e., area covered by the objects to be measured.

The first step outward from digit counting is usually

a 'model system' which corresponds to body-points with a fixed conventional order, and which is often nothing more than notched sticks or string-linked pebbles or bones, like rosary beads.

Soon three counting systems evolved: In the first, 'number' was indistinguishable from a physical object. To deal with quantities above four, concrete procedures were developed, including finger-counting and other body-counting procedures, keyed to a one-for-one correspondence and leading to the development of ready-made mappings accompanied by appropriate gestures.

In the second, the list of the names of the body parts in the established numerical order acquired abstract equivalencies and began to dissociate from the body parts. Then the abstractions became more attached to the corresponding number, and could be applied to new sets of objects.

In the third system, numerical nomenclature – or the fundamental names of the numbers – began to take shape.

For the Kara-Khaaks, concepts of mass and quantity generated from the body and remained fixed to notions of space filled and waiting to be filled, to notions of area. It becomes impossible to shift that conceptualizing with any kind of explanation or comparison. The ethnologists learned that we cannot possibly get inside another tribe's or people's entirely distinct concept of quantity without an explanation by them that forces us to adopt it, or forbids us from showing them why we cannot.

The Kara-Khaaks were a tribe whose concept of quantity had nothing to do with mass or units of a substance, but, rather only with how much ground the material covered: more 'of' something – say, wood – existed if it covered more ground than a smaller pile.

How could the anthropologists show that a vertical stack of 1,000 kilos of lumber was the same quantity as 1,000 kilos spread out? Running each pile through a scale and getting equal weight would, of course, be nonsensical to them. Their quantity contained a notion of measurement equally as sophisticated as that of their observers, but for the natives measurement was a kind of arrangement rather than a calibration.

The only way to illustrate quantitative identity would be to spread the vertical pile out to cover the same amount of ground surface as the original pile. But that would entail adopting their notion of quantity, or accomplishing an explanation only by letting them remain 'inside' their quantity-concept and not bringing them over to the observers'.

We might say that their quantity had a physicality that had not matured along the abstraction gradient to where it could be gauged by instrumentation. But instruments might have been irrelevant to their tribal practices, where there might have been no barter and no practice of acquiring more than one needs, meaning that no one would take more wood than required to build a house identical to everyone else's.

Notions of number and amount travel out from the body along a ripening ladder of abstraction, complexity, simplification or usefulness. But they travel only so far as social practices – or, as Wittgenstein called them, 'forms of life' – allow.

43

The Shaman on Set Theory, Games of Chance

The shamans warned the camp hands away from cards and throwing dice:

Games can become, because of their self-reference, an independent universe, a distraction from the seeking of perfection. If they are taken as a universe in themselves, what a meager universe that is. They begin and end with their own derivations and their rules are the products of other rules within their systems. Working through them leads not to clarity but to confusion, to brambles and thickets of contradiction. This is onanism. A thinking man's onanism, but something nevertheless that must be discarded.

It is the seeker's power, unaided by other men's handiwork,

that burns through tricks and sets and systems. Vision comes from *out* of the heart and from the heart's *looking outward*. Persist in this, gathering the past against itself to push you on, and you will find you have come to the spirits' plain, a hedged away and rock-encircled ground. You will recognize, for truly it is where you were meant to live – without design, without contrivance or prefiguration. The spirit's light is bursting-ripe and uncontained. You stand before it and raise your arms. It splits and spills like a blood moon over the fence's stones.

44

The Bird Inside

It was a normal evening for my wife and me, reading in separate rooms, or in the same room, not speaking. It was then that the bird came in, high above on the third floor, possibly through one of the tiny gable windows. There was a thump and a rustle, a thump and another rustle. We each looked up but not at each other.

The sound receded, muting a little in the peak rafters or maybe because the thing was tiring. Mixed in with the noise of hitting and feathers was an almost inaudible screech, possibly its chirping or the scraping of its feet against the plaster and windows. I knew how small a bird's brain was. It had to be a creature made almost purely of heart, a frantic little missile of will.

My wife turned the page. She had a special coolness that set in with interruptions.

The sounds returned to their former volume. Would the thing eventually die? I decided going up into either of the small rooms it had to be in would frighten it all the more, and might result in my getting hit. (My grandmother once had a bat fly in through her bedroom window and, in shooing it out, noticed its irritated, monkey-like face, which seemed to her the face of Satan.)

Finally there was silence. To my chagrin, my wife mounted the stairs with me. The first door we opened was the right one. It had gotten out. There were five or six feathers on the floor and marks, bloodless but faintly oily, on the wall where it had hit each time. The splotches glinted in the declining sunlight. My wife and I looked at each other. Then we turned to the small, chilly, evenly-lit square which whispered, out of all the others and without sound: *freedom*.

45

Aviateca

The coming of the Great Birds was not obvious, as people took the new patches of color on trees and hillsides to be weather-induced, strange colorations in the terrain caused by confusing atmospheric phenomena. The fowl were resting, heads nestled in feathers the passing people took for lambent, transfiguring leaves. Beaks and feet were also curled under, inert and branchlike, woven around the thickening autumnal barks and sap carbuncles and squirrel tunnels like innocuous new vines. Many of the brilliant swathes of feathers were close to one another. In other areas like the Mediterranean, one could drive one or two hundred miles before seeing the first incongruous patch.

The first calls came in the hours between midnight and dawn, in the weeks when the New Mars was smoldering and rolling away in the southwestern skies. Deep and prolonged, they seemed at their highest pitches absurd and loon-like, but reminded keepers of plow beasts or the mournful lowing of their buffalo.

The awakenings occurred all at once, spanning latitudes from the Crimean archipelago to the Bay of Odessa. Long necks rose slowly like snakes. The blinking eyelids were covered with dust and pieces of leaves. Turkish men in a cane pontoon thought it was the previous night's wine when the enormous, snow-bright, ruffling plumes and orange stilts of legs unfolded like new machinery across the road from their distilling cabins.

Groups of the beasts started gathering over the needleboat harbors of Dau, Sevastopol, Hidzju, Taganrog. Their mission had begun, not modest, of lifting all the shadows of that region of the earth. Long sheets of the light's absence were gathered up in their talons and hoisted. They took it out from under the passing clouds, from behind the girth of the capital's buildings, from the very abundance of trees that had served as their cradles. People gathered to watch the flocks of them bearing away the darkness like tarps. The people approved. Across the patches that had been cleared, the sun once again flung spangles, leaving the lee water sparkling like soda.

46

A Kingdom Road

Though we were making good progress on the only road north to the former *oblast* capital, the traffic problem was irritating. Our mission was to ascertain whether it was the True Dictator or the False Dictator our missile had destroyed, and the delay of an hour or two would have made no difference. But it was irritating, more precisely insulting, to encounter, in the wide open desert kingdom, in our specially-made vehicles, the kind of dead time we had to tolerate back home on the Southern California freeways.

We were waved around the stopped car by army personnel. Whether they were the well-paid and loyal True Army (black berets) or the less-well-paid and often surrendering False Army (berets of dark taupe), I had no way of knowing. Whoever was in the white car with its red interior had made it out. A great white tarp lay in front of the broken windshield, probably covering the pothole that had caused the car to stop so perilously. A can disclosing some kind of liquid with bobbing objects was sitting beside the open door.

The issue, then, was whether the first missiles we had launched had killed the True Dictator. Everyone knew that the one certainty, besides cruelty, that could be expected from the True Dictator was his proliferation of doubles – False Dictators – to draw inquiry, reconnaissance and, ultimately if need be, fire and bombardment upon themselves. In the regime's dizzying logic, the one truism remained that the False should be sacrificed for the True.

After the great missile strike, a dictator had come on television. He looked to be false. His fuller jowls and unprecedented eyewear were more redolent of a flustered spinster than an aging, septuagenarian tribesman.

Imagine our horror when the news came over the dash fax just as we reached the city's outskirts. It was war, and everyone had been wrong. The generals who had turned on him had been waving us around the roadblock. A separate missile had exploded in front of the car and spun it around. The steering wheel pierced the driver's sternum and he – the True One – had gone through the windshield and was under the tarp, again in the manner of a grubby stateside mishap.

Someone had been trying to clean off the seats of the car, which were actually white. It was sponges that had been bobbing in the bucket of bloody water.

47

Unravelling

I'm a Luddite. So sue me. I drive a cab in Novosibirsk. But I'm starting to get a little worried. I pushed the cassette rewind button in the car yesterday and it not only rewound but *erased* the tape, and then erased the CD in the compartment above it. By, say, mile six or seven, the digital numerals on the tracking selection screen were gone, and then the numbers on the clock – zip, zip, zip into invisibility, into the brimming fucking void. I looked up at the rearview and it had vanished, but I compensated with the side mirror. Guess what? I was without any rear vision in the automobile, nothing but my craning, now profusely sweating neck. The left front fender of the Lada started eating itself away into the air, as if gone over by a giant pencil eraser, a good five feet of pure sunlight taking out what had been a flank of British racing green. The hood ornament erased itself with the circular movement in which it was no doubt fashioned. What would be next? The wheels? The seat I was sitting in, or the steering column? The hood came off without vanishing, just rose up like a cellar door in a movie tornado. Who knew what pieces of the engine and drive line were going. More stuff came off, so much that it flew away like bird feathers, buckshot hitting a blasted crow. I was left with seat and steering wheel, turning onto Ulitsa Leninskaya with what should have been flashes of panic but which, given the venue, was simply embarrassment. What is a man without a car in this city? Ten times the man who can't *even keep his car coherent* in less than a neighborhood's distance of windless driving. I tipped the valet. He was astonished. I brushed off my suit and left the small crowd gathering about the floating wheel and seat.

48

Dostoevsky's House, Novokuznetsk

The Grand Inquisitor had it that the Devil tempted Christ in the wilderness with three questions. The first was the question of food, the question of bread. As the Maker and the Maker's son and the man of miracles, He was as susceptible as His flock to the first temptation. It was simple. Christ could offer the multitudes bread in exchange for their freedom, and once the yearning for freedom was gone an earthly kingdom of peace could be assured. 'There is no crime and therefore no sin; there is only hunger,' the Devil said. 'Give man food, and then ask of him virtue.'

And how subtle, how amazing is this temptation. Loving His people this much, wouldn't He want for them this most basic of satisfactions? And wouldn't it be easiest for them to take? With food they could get – the people of, say, Magadan could get – at least over into the following day. They could worry about freedom when the right time came. Life had to be there first, before they could think how to live.

But the temptation would not be had. Bread was renounced, and freedom chosen. Legend has it that the Devil ran away cackling into the woods and Christ, His mouth frozen in the perfect circle of his 'no', appeared to cover it for a second with the hand he lifted, as if in doubt.

49

Talismanic Object

By the early fifteenth century, the Russians had triumphed over the Tartars but still had no state, no clearly defined land borders. Sacred art was the obsessive vehicle of a national identity in the absence of a *polis*. What kept Russians together was their Christianity, and what kept Christianity together, besides the liturgies and rituals of the Mass, was the constant refinement and elevation of the icon.

These gilt and lacquered plates were held above the lines of battle as talismans, vessels of holy will that covered movements and decisions with a supernatural force-field. The icon was, like the dove, a paraclete, a receptacle of the Godhead and its earthly realization in the forward progress of the Christian army. To the wounded and dying, the absence of a priest would never matter so long as the icon was nearby. It was kissed, touched, held to the head; it shone like a chalice above the dust and blood.

50

Weapons of the
Steppe People

Burial Mound, Hermitage Museum

Etched up by the hilt of the sword: the name of the Uzbek *khan*, and mottos in a fiery, brazen nomenclature. Heft enough to split an aspen out of its trunk, but still a nimble tip for hollowing the antler bone to nozzles for the whistling arrows: tens of thousands of white missiles people heard from far away. It was a rising cry, the Song of Death: *Just as the flower under the Volga storm, who rises up against this is erased.*

51

Heavenly City, Earthly City

The convent's palace, four hundred years old, called Lopukhin, smooth and faded red and sunset orange. Peter the Great's first wife moved here after he died and she left the Suzdal convent, where he had sent her when he was tired of her. The green-roofed house, its top floors paced in the night by the widows of Tsar Theodore. Napoleon's guards tried to blow it up, but the nuns snuffed out the fuses.

The clouds two miles up seem close to the onion cupolas and frozen, twisted tents of wood. Large cats and stones in the courtyard. Sparrows chirp and hop in the freezing gravel. Always, swiftly from door to door and over the long yards, the tall, quick monks.

52

Heavenly City,
Earthly City II

The convent's reflection blazes in the pond that lies before it. The long wall has filigreed dips as sturdy as gun notches, and the white mortar sparkles between the bricks. The domes of the church, topped by two-tiered, bent-cross, arched crucifixes, have turned from copper to dark moss green, each wrapping its arms around the posts of heaven. Banners of all the orders flap and bells resound and stop, resound and stop. In the cemetery, busy, ominous headstones: Chekhov (aged forty-one), Gogol, Prokofiev and Shostakovich. Fyodor Chaliapin singing under the ground like real Orpheus now. In the corner, under the largest, most pugnacious stone: a single man, Ukrainian and pious. Khruschev, with the accent on the second syllable. The grave untended and unvisited.

53

Sphinx

We were living in Abakan in 2003, preparing to head out to Katanda and the Ukok Plateau, Khazakstan border regions in the southern mountain ranges of the Altai. These were places of unimaginable beauty and, without proper precaution, almost certain disease.

There was a new variant of mefloquine in the US. It had always been the 'miracle' drug for malaria, its own side effect being vivid but fairly harmless hallucinations or 'rapid dreams' that filled the opiated naps it tended to induce. The epidemiologist in New York hadn't told me this.

I had stretched out on a wicker chaise on our screened balcony and washed the third pair of spansules down with a glass of *kvas*, grainy and thick as Turkish coffee.

The beast appeared before me, enormous and

stationary, floating like a giant kite in the humid air outside the porch window. I was looking at its underside, a belly of thick brown fur, coarse and sticky, as though dripping with creosote. The head was triangular, more insect than mammal. Its mouth was an empty mask-like hole, but there was also a proboscis, a dazzling rhino horn of flaming orange and deep indigo.

When it finally moved, I saw enormous eyes: rotund and shining, translucent with the film that glistened down the bearish abdomen. It finally lifted itself away with a racket, like some primitive, malfunctioning machine.

I wrote to the doctor when I got down to Ulan Bator. He answered back that yes, indeed, there had been tales of distortions, monstrous transformations of objects the patient in fact was actually seeing.

I hadn't been sleeping. The fly had rested on the screen only a second or two before whisking away. I had never even really shut my eyes.

54

Sea Swords

Magadan. The place of the great blue icebergs, the far Northeast's true and only ship's graveyard. Some of them miles long, though the deadliest only a thousand or two meters, flung like scimitars by the crosscurrents and tsunamis. All of them low-lying, quietly deadly, like submarines: no upper mass to be seen until the moon's glint catches their great barge-body, and if no moon the black sword's cross-cut slash. A crunch. The rivets and steel plates springing apart, splintering acres of metal. Explosion after white explosion. Many a convict ship was lost this way, as if the navy guards who loaded the prisoners knew in advance.

55

The Log

Of all the fanciful varieties of extermination, God have mercy on those who got the log. This was a true Kafkaesque mechanism, the machine from the penal colony whittled down to a single railroad tie. The Soviets used them in camps where mills had high escarpments for building timber chutes and current-powered water wheels. These high hills were accessible only by layers of steps, usually eighteen or twenty to a tier, tier groups of five or six or ten at the most. One camp in Perm 7 had a hill of three hundred steps. Each was kept brushed of its surface snow so its nearly constant base of ice glimmered brownly like a sutured wound down the mountainside.

The prisoner was tied to the log and simply let go. He spun out into an infinity of wind and thunderous clumping. Like hanging, the blame could be laid upon his own weight and mass and the unforgiving leveler of gravity. The body, even the head, was always found intact, the ropes having held tidily even when the tie itself splintered. The prisoner was usually dead by the third or fourth tier of steps. To Muslims, he was seen as a sort of tragic negative dervish, spinning from Being off into oblivion: 'Back to the Nowhere from out of the Here.'

56

Arrival of the Kulaks

They were sentenced to the Eastern camps for enriching themselves, amassing horses and barns and workers to help them till the pastureland. All private property acquisition had become, certainly by the late twenties, intrinsically anti-Soviet, so the mood among them was of a people who had lost all hope of regaining their freedom. This fostered deep enmity towards the regime, and the authorities, knowing this full well, kept the powerful repressive machine at the ready. The *kulak* exiles then lived by the same laws of survival and accommodation as the rest of the country under Stalin.

Living conditions varied greatly for different groups of labor settlers. In general, the famine and mass deaths of the early period of special exile were gone, but the majority of labor settlers, as well as free citizens, still faced enormous hardships. NKVD reports themselves mentioned inadequate barracks and dugouts, and a complete lack of schools and hospitals. At the same time, the endurance and tenacity of the former *kulaks* allowed them not only to survive but live fairly well and, in some cases, achieve a high level of comfort by Soviet standards. Among the agricultural cooperatives there were several 'millionaire *kolkhozy*'– well-off farms which irritated the local authorities.

57

Yagoda's Idea

A sadist of enormous appetite, he himself had killed his predecessor Yezhov, and was Stalin's architect of the Sovietized camp system. Their conversion into colonization settlements came largely from this April 1930 memorandum:

To Comrades Eikhe, Messing, Yevdokimov:

The question of the camps must be resolved from a different perspective. Today the camp is a mere gathering of inmates, whose labor we use without any prospects for either the inmates or ourselves. It is essential to make labor more voluntary by giving the inmates more freedom after work. We have to convert the camps into colonization settlements without waiting for the conclusion of prison terms. Reducing a sentence for good behavior, out of philanthropic impulse, is unacceptable and often quite harmful. This also gives the wrong impression that the inmate has been rehabilitated and a hypocritical notion of good behavior, which may be suitable for bourgeois states, but not for us. The whole purpose of transferring inmates to us is to liquidate prisons. It is clear that, under the existing system, their liquidation will take many years, because a camp *per se* is worse than prison. We have to colonize the North in the shortest possible time.

Here is my plan: All inmates should be transferred to settlements until the end of their terms. Do it this way: a group (1,500 people) of selected inmates from different regions – give them lumber and offer to build huts for them to live in. Those willing to bring families should be allowed to do so. [They will be] controlled by a warden, in a settlement of 200–300 houses. During their spare time, after the lumbering season, they (especially the weak) will work in vegetable gardens, raise pigs, mow grass, and fish. At first they will survive on rations, and later – on their own. The settlement could be expanded by adding exiles. There are colossal deposits of natural resources there: oil and coal, for instance. I am sure that, years from now, these settlements will become proletarian mining towns. Today our prisoners are, for the most part, agriculturalists. They are attracted to land. We now have very few guards and very few escapes. Women should be allowed to settle and marry. It should be done immediately. We have to find enthusiastic people capable of turning the entire prison system upside down; it has become thoroughly rotten.

A month later, the Politburo decided to build a canal between the White and Baltic Seas using convict labor. The first large project entrusted to the OGPU, it would involve 276,000 workers, administrative personnel, guards and service providers. It would become the largest futile public works program in the history of the modern world.

58

Descendents of the Kat People

At a pond on the tundra, an old man and woman in the hut they reached by reindeer cart. Their fishing hole covered with hides that let through their lines, their stools of the same hide, supported by crossed birch sawhorses cut so new their chips and sap smell fresh. The only other smell their kerosene lantern, Sobranie cigarettes. She wears a scarf of several layers, something gossamer on a kind of fleece or seal hide, and he an earmuffed cap with a pointed top, like soldiers' underhelmets from early Soviet times. A .22/.410 over/under gun leans up against the doorway to ward off poachers, wolves, to kill a truly massive pike that will not die by the gaff.

His face, he says, has cracks for every road he traveled

in each of the early forest camps. Her skin still as smooth as butter, she could be his daughter or granddaughter. Their children have moved to Novosibirsk and do not write or visit. Their pets have died and their pensions have dried up. Their friends have started to follow each other down to their graves and under the ground. The wife says she imagines them fishing now under the ice, their lines falling down from the unseen to the seen world as moon rays, specks of starlight, willow branches that sometimes rise up from the hole.

Somehow religion, or at least the subject of priests, comes up. She takes a long drag of Balkan tobacco smoke, sighs and lets it out. She looks at the hut wall as if it contained a window.

'The orthodox bishop in Krasnoyarsk should be helping us, but he doesn't. He's hostile. He works for the secret police. Has for years. Trying to preach in Russia now is like speaking to a country hit by the atom bomb. It's been laid to waste for two generations. It's worse than working among heathens. The only source of hope is the children and old women. (She nodded to me to indicate she did not consider herself one.) 'The rest are blind. The villages are dying. They are paying for everything that happened.

59

Night Rainbow

They do exist. Goyen looked out the Tupelov window and saw one bending over the sawtooth distance of the Baikal range. The moon not only had to be full, but the sky exceptionally cloudless and bright for enough light to bring the hues out of a band of mist. A rainy day's treasure blooming like this in the night's vacuity: it made Goyen feel blessed on the earth, the recipient of gifts of some animist god. He'd seen one years before in America, in Portland, and no one believed him then. But the valley below it was ugly, shipyard-and-barge-and-dirty-water crowded. Here it looked like a gate to the whites of Heaven. The mountains stood under it silently, attentive, like columns of giants.

60

The Judgment

There was supposed to be an old Soviet judge who was impotent save for the moment he passed sentences, at which time he ejaculated violently and copiously. His head would dip and his eyes flicker after his pronouncements, so much so that the magistrate stenographer considered walking up and nudging him back to cogency with a glass of water. I only know this from old writers in the Moscow bureaus of American magazines. The passing of death sentences (then all done by firing squads and still in Lubyanka) would send him into paroxysms, a surging and buzzing such as might come from an over-volted table lamp. There would be a softening, some would say a deepening, of the voice. Then unexpected pauses. He would stare beyond the heads of prisoners and counsel and up into the audience, with a gaze that bore through them as though into a radiating grid of infinity, a sort of honeycomb of consolation. With respect to professional articles, his specialty was in the great punishments of mythology: Sisyphus and his rock, the torments of Prometheus. The Hades ravens tearing Orpheus into pieces and dropping his head to bob on the purple water, mouth still moving, singing to Apollo. He imagined that what those executed experienced was no more than the way he felt in the fourteenth, fifteenth, seventeenth second of his ravishment: tranquil and dispersed, sprinkled upon the tide of something vast and musical.

61

The Black Hand

Goyen went into a clinic in Irkutsk for some antihistamines. His entire maxillary sinus felt as though it were packed with ice and gravel. On the gurney on the other side of the curtain from him was a hysterical army private, still whacking his hair. The Ixodes ticks had dropped on him from the overhead bin in the train compartment. Everyone knew about the ticks; warnings and disclaimers embellished every guidebook. The ticks invariably carried encephalitis, paralyzing the neck and limbs and possibly crippling the victim for life.

The soldier was still in his fatigues, his head shaking back and forth and his unwashed hair standing up in wild patches like rooster feathers. The doctors were preoccupied with more serious cases, though Goyen could appreciate the seriousness of the soldier's situation.

Whenever a nurse or orderly walked by, he stopped his thrashing and lay silent for a second, then reached out stiffly for the passing white gown. His sleeves were rolled up and he mimicked what he thought the ticks had done to him, boring with his fingers down into the underside of his forearm.

Later Goyen learned how assiduous was the anti-Chinese prejudice of border soldiers like his fellow patient. The recruit had apparently gone into convulsions, though there was no real indication he'd even been bitten. He'd told his doctor the ticks were the size of spiders, with tiny earnest yellow faces and slanted eyes. Their black fur had become the snapped-up green woolen caps of the Chinese militia. He had even seen a red star on the top of one of them.

After Goyen got his prescription, dispensed in a small brown packet that doubled as a drinking cup, he walked out into the clinic yard to look for a water fountain. He looked down the mountainside toward Lake Baikal, the rocky hillocks whistling and rattling with millions of fallen birch leaves. There was bracken, fungus, whirtleberries, and stands of new-generation pine and spruce, but they only served as small patches on the great garment of birches that ran for miles out to the zenith on all sides of the water. The undropped part of their canopy nestled together like shaggy, grazing beasts in the mountains' shadows. The bare trunks standing in front of him creaked in the breeze like masts.

62

Paraclete

It was a good omen getting into our daughter's birth city and seeing, first thing, the Spasso-Proebrazhensky Cathedral. It had survived not just the man-made extremes of Soviet vilification, but also the natural ones: floods and earthquakes, forest fires that exploded around it like tinder under the torch of the autumn suns. The Cheka had dragged patriarchs out by their hair and beaten them unconscious with icons, setting fire to their robes and beards. Wings of the cathedral had been earmarked for a Museum of Atheism, but the cupolas had never been touched, and were faithfully repainted their gold pastel year after year. Their six spires were six spear points held steady against the void, the infidel, the Hordes that might slip southward and put the knife to an otherwise unguarded, placid people.

Inside, the altars and icons had their normal gold and silver, brass and tin and copper for lesser exhibits and water-bearing vessels. There were fountains of plain white stone and wooden wall-marker graves for the resting places of the bishopric. But this was Siberia, the land of mines, and this particular earth's materials were foregrounded no less than the silver in the Taxco churches of Mexico. Here were miniature chimneys of tin for the burning of waste, walls of thick-pressed gypsum, statues of basalt and chunks of chromium ore in glass cubes that seemed something out of a natural-history museum. The God of this place was a God of stones and minerals, a deity of the building blocks of things, the elements.

There was so much rock and metal inside that my footsteps were louder than in any place I'd ever been. It was though a tape of echoes had been set up in loudspeakers, building in overlapping cracks to the point where I took off my boots, carrying the big Cabellas around my neck joined by their strings. I remembered this was the city where mica was mined, the brittle, glittery stuff I'd seen shining from the sidewalks of Hollywood Boulevard. Buryat and Yenisei peoples had panned it out of rivers long before the industrialized Russians built their little rail tunnels and brought it up in buckets. I thought of the mine I had seen the day before, its entry timbers collapsed and plunged into still-flooded pits.

There was mica everywhere, and I ran my hand along

the banisters where the translucent flakes had fallen from high vestibules. Their little shards ran through my fingers like pieces of the sky itself, a crumbling substance of air and cloud. The sun shafts in the open spaces above me were filled with mote-sized bits of it, floating as purely and evenly as particles of light. I slapped the shoulder of my jacket and a puff came up, like manna traveling back from where it had come. Weeks later, in LA, flakes of it sprayed out of my pockets when I undressed. There, of course, it had lost its sacred cast and seemed like broken pieces of tinsel.

63

She-devil,
Timber Camp at Omsk

The lumbermen saw her after much drinking of grain alcohol (not vodka).

Her mechanical black and silver body had a plastic rectangular box at its center. Inside were stacks of bark and steel marbles scattered like ball bearings. Wires ran through and served as veins: red, green, bright blue and yellow, and some completely transparent, whose open possibility of the transmission of anything seemed the most frightening. She was like an Archimboldo portrait constructed of numerous elements, but all of them the opposite of flowers, fruit, food – whatever the Italian painter would have deemed repellent. Her face was half a grinning skull, half radio grille with low-lit tuning dial.

Her head was crowned with additional wires as fine as matted twine shards, possibly steel wool. Her forearms were saw pulleys, the elbows bent and oiled and squealing with ropes. Her fingers were awl-thin crosscut saws, dust-caked, smudged with iron filings, emerging and retracting in silent unison. There were earrings: cut-off human thumbs and toes and noses in tiny vials of formaldehyde; insect larvae from the sawdust piles preserved in amber, white sectioned bodies and black dots of eyes agleam. Her hands held terrible antiquated obstetric instruments, the tools of abortionists and *gulag* novice torturers. Her lips were blinding bright – aluminum, the watchers gathered – and were retracted, peeled severely back from pearl-white wolf or coyote incisors. She wore, like Kali herself, a necklace of tiny skulls, mice or weasels or wood lizards, and a belt of severed human hands she'd gathered from the table saws, their puddles of blood stringing from stump to stump in crimson trails of slime. The tips of the chopped hands' fingers were dried and rustled like leaves.

Her feet were coalcart wheels from the furnace room, squeaking, inching forward with prosthetic uncertainty. Greenish-white crystals sprinkled from her armpits, glittering spikes of silica falling in calcified stalactites.

The men saw her once, twice, three times, floating in front of the enormous vertical saw. It served as the axis of her back, a slowly pumping iron spine of bright half-moons. Each sighting made them stay away for days, drinking more, afraid of sleep. Had they been their ancestors they would have gathered offerings, which would have been themselves.

64

The Map-reader

Goyen looked at the map of Siberia spread out on the empty cafeteria table of the Hotel Kuzbass. The Northeast, sprawling like an unexplored, lounging maiden under the Arctic and Laptev Seas, was five times the size of France and narrowed to a drape of icy hair that hung down over cowering Japan. It was a serious mass, Siberia. A daunting, no-nonsense chunk of the planet's net territory.

He knew these places had the lowest recorded temperatures in the inhabited Northern Hemisphere. It was a cold that gobbled you whole, a toothless set of gums like a whale's that rolled and pressed you with fumbling indifference into the grave. He thought with pride of his knowledge of Robert Frost, and noted that while Hitler had chosen fire as his method of extermination, Stalin had certainly opted for ice.

He was transfixed by the notion of beauty set down in the midst of so much suffering, like pinholes of light in the grey, sagging roof of a circus tent. The radiance, the flower fields, the isolated monasteries would have to be searched for. He had been reading Shalamov's *Kolyma Tales*, in which children were found in drifts with necks snapped like dandelions, workers frozen by their labors were simply added to log piles, and missing men from the morning gang tallies were easily assumed to be dead rather

than escaped. His favorite story was 'Prosthetic Devices', where every prisoner had to hand in fiberglass arms and legs for security checks, and the final prisoner, the only whole-bodied one, says: 'You can't have my soul.'

Goyen flattened the creases of the map. He would Hellenize the place in his chosen manner – a photography journal, a series of sketches, *frissons* of some sort. He took one of the cigars from the box I had given him during his unexplained tour of the orphanage. He tilted them and they rolled toward the front, the tight-packed tubes rattling. The East was built of bones as surely as Petersburg.

A chill went through him at the sound, tempering his vanity, reminding him of the solemnity of his task.

He believed in omens like this, portents. He blew smoke rings which widened, making room for others he blew inside them, filling the centers over and over. Outside, through the smoke, he watched the scattered Vs of birds moving upwards toward the clouds.

65

God as a Child

I read to my daughter the old northern legend of how God created the *taiga* when He was still a child. There weren't many colors, but they were childishly fresh and vivid, and their subjects were simple.

Later, when God grew up and became an adult, He fashioned more complex patterns from colored pages – like the cut-outs of Matisse – and his creation was populated by many-hued animals and flamboyant birds. By then, He had grown bored by His former child's world and threw snow on His forest creations, traveling south toward the heat of India, uncertain whether He would ever return.

My daughter, *moya docha*, lifted her hands toward the simpler designs in the illustration *en face* to the text. Looking up from her crib, she favored the black

stick figures laying across the snow like simple Chinese characters on an ivory scroll. It was as if she could tell this was the world's starting place, the mind's very backbone, the region in which creation and permission began.

66

The Wait

All parents adopting in Russia must do so in two trips. This results from many things: traditional Soviet distrust of foreigners; the glacial movement of any Russian bureaucracy; suspicion of documentation; and recently, well-supported stories of child-trafficking in former Soviet republics like Georgia, Moldova and Ukraine.

So three weeks after our first trip, when Putin issues a new decree lengthening a child's time on a registry from three to six months, we are stuck in the middle. Did the six months commence at the time of the first visit, the time the decree was signed or, God forbid, the time you see the baby on the second, normally final 'pick-up' visit? The latter would mean a third trip to actually retrieve a child you might have met six months to a year before. And again, you'd hope for the law not to change and start the time running all over again.

Somehow, we slip under the radar. The orphanage gets the Education Ministry to run the three months from our first visit's end (late December '04), so our daughter is counted as being back on for three months by the time we go in to get her on 1 March.

But she has been 'hidden' for us by Elena, the social service worker. Her name was on the registry, but the orphanage mothers promise to stow her away, even if she is asked for by name. She is like Anne Frank in an imaginary attic; in the new language of the auto thugs, they 'keep her out of the showroom'.

Other couples, everywhere we go, prove far less lucky. Some have second pick-up trips slated for their baby's removal from the three-month list, only to be forced with the choice of returning home or being stranded in a Russian city for several months. And these are cold places, with artificially high hotel prices: Khabarovsk, Yakutsk, Vladivostok. Five-hour, seven-hour plane journeys from Moscow.

You can tell, when you see them in hotels later with their kids, that the blood is nearly drained from these parents. They wobble, fatigued beyond belief. They do not trust their power to stay awake and get the job done.

But of course the worst are the ones who have arrived the second time but cannot pick up the babies they have bonded with on the first trip. That initial 'selection' journey is pivotal; it sets all the machinery of the heart in motion. The link has been built. Then, only hours, days afterward, a worse void sets in than the one pre-existing the entire process. It is the void of having, then having the given thing snatched away. Clutching one's offspring at last and then watching them sealed off, locked in a vast room of stampers and shufflers.

These adoptive parents, these people stand in emptiness. They are shells lit from within by a fitful, crackling, buzzing wire of yearning. Hope is still in them, but in its lowest and last flicker. They are like the people in séances with their hands on cups, waiting for the hint of a pull. They want the spirit back in the room, but know that things greater than spirit block the way.

67

Orphanage

From the outside, the orphanage had the usual first bad signs: cobwebs in the front door corners, cracked window glass held together only by its honeycomb of wire. But inside, turning left at the boot bench, the long yellow hall and ceiling glowed with tiny, cheerful industry. Walking past the waist-high kitchen opening, our faces caught in the silver of the pans, ballooned in reflection and then disappearing. The women cooks – there were no men, this is not the land of men – were baking bread in their tall paper hats. The pounding of my heart increased. My wife was eight or ten steps behind me, turning around and around at the walls of children's drawings.

We sat in the director's tiny office. She had a tough-dame look she wore like a relic from Soviet times. She read us the health stats of the mother, the father's occupation, height and surprising non-dependence on alcohol. My wife ran her long nail down the columns, the pediatrician we'd hired sitting between us asking questions of the director, nodding with encouragement.

The orphanage doctor appeared in the doorway with our daughter, lifting her diapered bottom in her palm as if she were a light bulb about to be changed. The doctor turned her to the right and left, the baby's blue eyes sparkling, wandering. My wife yelped and the room burst into laughter. The baby laughed. The pediatrician pulled approvingly at his long red beard, unwound his stethoscope from his neck and patted my hand.

68

Payday

Though they had lived and worked hard at the East Ural Mensk smeltery throughout the Soviet times, the workers had no idea how bad the barter payment system would become when the Kremlin ran out of cash in Yeltsin's first year. The workers had been paid before in potatoes, fuel oil, automobile parts and general food and staples vouchers. The idea was that you could trade these on the black market for currency or truly wanted goods at a very slight commission.

But in the fall of 91 people started coming away from the paycheck line with boxes of costume jewelry, leather goods that were neither belts nor gloves nor boots, and bag after oversized bag of Scandinavian dildos. The dildo sacks were doubly insulting given their elongated size (like kitchen garbage bags) and the fact they were invariably of clear plastic. Also, the devices were multicolored: not just pale and black, but red, yellow, brown and some even transparent themselves, with tiny internal bubbles like soda water or the clear marbles of childhood.

Dildos were problematic on the black market. Rubber dealers could melt them down, but these merchants were inundated and severely backlogged. Rosa and Ludmilla wanted to drag the bags down the hill to the market square, but modesty forced them to wrap pages of *Pravda* around them to make them look like bundles of flowers. The women blamed their own government, of course, but also excoriated the population of Northern Europe. The Danes, Swedes and Finns, the women agreed, were a genuinely pathetic people: How could life consist solely of these sexual acrobatics? No work, no pastimes, not even eating or sleeping.

Ludmilla peeked in over the folded paper, and gasped when she noticed one with a double head. Rosa agreed that it had some type of medical or prosthetic utility. Rosa marveled at the detail in the light-colored ones: the green and blue veins, the soft ridges of the head and testicles. It had been many, many years ago for her. Her husband was a naval officer whose ardor had dissipated drastically after Brezhnev.

The market line in front of the rubber dealer's kiosk ran all the way down to the Ufa River, and little side markets were forming given the variety of dildo materials: plastic, which could be melted down faster, and wood, which the firewood boys would gladly splinter into inoffensive kindling.

Not wanting to endure further examination, the two women concluded theirs were of standard rubber, and went to the end of the line and sat on their bags. They pulled their scarves around their heads and listened to the swift water flowing behind them. All up the hill toward the stalls, younger workers – mainly women and high-school girls – sat shamelessly on their bags playing cards and drinking, though it was not yet noon.

Rosa pulled out a cigarette her husband had rolled for her. She tried to distract herself with admiration for its fine handiwork, the military crispness of the smooth paper and tamped ends. But looking up the line of the hill, at the brown mud and dust of the riverbank and surrounding mountains, she noticed something. The dildo bags were the only colored things she could see. They were like a hedge of flowers dividing the blacks and browns that pressed down on them in their daily walks to work. The pattern they made was glorious and fresh, vivid, ravishing as any summer garden.

69

Door into the Dark

However effective and earnest their efforts – and these are people of extraordinary diligence, of superhuman kindness and decency – the orphanage women are fighting against a future that will fall on their unadopted charges like a Ural avalanche. The economy is disintegrating, marriage has been down two decades and divorce rates are skyrocketing. When a tyrannical yoke descends on a people, it frays the familial bonds because it corrodes trust, supplants all ties of blood (children turning in parents during the purges, etc). When the yoke lifts as it did fifteen years ago, the economy convulses properly or improperly into its privatized life.

But the restoration of families takes longer. The belief that a spouse owes something to another spouse, or that children should be grateful to parents – all of this rests on the notion of family as the conceptual bedrock of morality, something Soviet life undercut from the first Communards. As a result, lovers freely beat one another in drinking sprees, people are careless about birth control, cavalier about raising their offspring. It goes back to the camp mentality of living only for the day you occupy. Caretaking as a state function rather than that of blood kindred, this is what you see on the streets every day. The orphanage system has some 500,000 adoptive children now, the vast majority over the age of three.

When this happens, in any society, the chance of a child being adopted drops exponentially with every year of age. As vast as the sea of infertile searchers is in the West, the market evaporates quickly for anyone north of a toddler.

You can see it in the eyes of the caretakers, and most devastatingly, in the eyes of primary and secondary schoolchildren.

A colleague of ours on the magazine adopted girl siblings, five and seven, at the same time we adopted our baby daughter. These girls were classic, post-Soviet abandoned urchins, found eating out of a dumpster when they were five and three. As good as the orphanage schools are, neither could recognize even half the letters of either the Roman or Cyrillic alphabets. They had never been out of Yaroslavl, never even *into* that city from the air force base where the orphanage stood. They had never been in an automobile or on an airplane, let alone taken a seventeen-hour trip to San Francisco. Unadopted boys head out to the world of petty and mafia crime – arms and drug running, auto parts ventures with the Chechens. For girls, it's the brothels and escort services, sometimes as early as fourteen or fifteen.

Their new father told us there was a moment in a day three or four weeks after they got back when he could see that the girls knew, really *saw*, that they had made it out of cold hell, out of the thicket. They had won the lottery, and they walked up a hillside in the Presidio and picked their mother handfuls of wildflowers.

70

Feeding Time

On the way in, we saw some kind of hardy potted flowers lining the stairs that rose to the boot bench: geraniums perhaps, snapdragons, something geranium-like at any rate. Then the long labor of removing boots, like pulling sections of pipe off of one's legs.

The chirping voices blew forward in a wave, but with each sound then dispersing, taking on a different tone, and slowly, as the women came through with the bottles, snuffing themselves out with the rapid *chug chug chug* of incessant sucking.

There is so little in the world we trust. It starts with the breast, or, for these many, all given away, the bottle. It starts with a square of thin blanket and the bed's iron bars —unpleasant to hit yourself against but guarding your fall, the first house, the first shelter. Protective matter.

One by one they fall asleep, and though we are not allowed to film anyone other than our daughter, we walk past rows of identical infants in piles of blankets so fresh the perfume of their detergent hits you like a warm wall of register heat. All week on the road here, we heard new stories of terrorist chatter on the cell phones. It hangs over our thoughts like smog, like poison gas. Now this uniform buzzing of baby's sleep, a holy drift of infusing peace. It is the sound of love itself. Innocence, satiety and comfort: the wolf banished, the bear of consciousness chased away.

What *are* these flowers, I ask myself again on the bench, lacing my boots. *Ne znayu*, says a caretaker: I don't know. In the pale afternoon light they are crisp and vivid under the freshet of their leaking window ledge. All their blossoms are pink or coral, small buds of tongues thrust up at the dripping ice.

149

71

Birch Borders

The birches ringing the orphanage building bright with ice, a drape of splintered glass that weighs the branches down and holds the black-and-white striped trunks inside a watery, wobbling scrim. These trees keep the cutter's chop-saw busy. Birches keep the wind off the playground. This is a realm of blacks and whites and their cognates only, no surge of cardinal red in the sheer gray sameness.

In spring the sun, the breeze, some somnolent magnetism brings the green back out. The leaves fall over one another's tiny blades like the growing scales of pangolins.

Hopscotchers and stickballers, boys playing soccer dodge in and out of the swaying caves the trees have formed. If the sun appears, the world is doubled with shadows. But again this second order of things is gray. No color is added. Nature is a miser here, delivering slowly, stingily on its promises. The white bark wears black bands; it is decorated by its own incipient absence. All that is worked upon recedes, lies fallow or stays invisible. The woodpecker pecks, but the hole does not appear.

72

One Out of Many

The orphanage babies are attended to uniformly, all at once or not at all. There is little individual attention. It is all quite Soviet, or excessively disciplinary, something over and above normal orphanage life. If one baby starts crying, the caregivers do not go in, but wait for her to tire. If the crying one wakes the others, the whole, onrushing wave is left to hiss and wash itself away, back into the inevitable tide of sleep. After eating, they are put on their potties immediately and kept there for a reasonable time, whether or not anything is produced. TV time, *Teletubbies* and so forth, is the same for everyone. Baths are communal, washing and drying a flurry of spiked hair and buffing towels. No one sings to the solitary sleepless crier. The voices are always a conglomeration, a chorus that starts and ceases together.

But this is supposed to be the time of ego-building, when consciousness starts to fortify itself by isolation, establishing domains. A baby learns, forgets, then learns again that its limbs are its own. If a hundred hands are raised in the air, whatever happens to the rest does not help the individual hand-holder. Cause and effect, control of the body, must be learned by the solitary owner of the thing to be controlled. It is visceral and not cerebral knowledge.

My daughter's eyes are blue as cobalt, 'early and instant blue', as Elizabeth Bishop said of her lover's eyes. She grips my thumb with amazing strength. She has *Sibirskoe zdorovye* , 'Siberian health'. At one time these were the growing fields of the mass man, and in ways, at least with child rearing, they still are. The mass can take in the flailing, sinking member and not be changed. So selfishly, or selflessly for her, I read her grip as craving uniqueness. She is the hardy, lost one in the corner of the field. *I am*, says the lamb on its buckling knees. *I am only one, I am only this.*

73

Ice Amber

Out of the orphanage city and east to Lake Baikal, which is so deep it contains a sixth of all the world's fresh water. Under layers of ice as clear as picture windows the staple animals of the region drift slowly or sleep, coming out of holes they remember with bat-like telepathy for food and air. There are *omul*, the pike-like fish that is the lakesmen's true livelihood. Like pike, they cry – actually *growl* – when lifted to the surface. They spawn upriver but return by November, when Baikal freezes. The sturgeons here weigh a quarter-ton, and carry twenty pounds of caviar each in their wombs. They, too, are true fighters at the hook, unlike the sturgeons of the river deltas who get stuck in shallows among roots and between the boots of chasing teenagers.

But Baikal is best known for the oddity of its animals,

hundreds of species unique to the lake alone, like some kind of cold-weather version of the Amazon or Dr Seuss's *On Beyond Zebra*. To look through the ice window is to turn the pages of a dictionary of imaginary creatures. There is a giant, shrimp-like crustacean called the 'Baikal horse' whose claws constantly grip two round stones, like a keel growing out of its belly. In summer, they wash up on the banks and dodge the scores of species of shore and forest birds that are found nowhere else on earth. But usually the 'horse' is safe – summer is short here. It is its own perfected paradise: an Eden, but a refrigerated Eden.

A mile down, well out of sight, are thousands of tiny, red-eyed *gammarid* shrimp. A tenth of the size of the horses, they guide themselves in banks of twisting, blinking pink, scuffing the tops of underwater mountains whose slopes go down another 3,000 feet. The water is kept pure, shade after deepening shade of aquamarine, by crabs that eat away the coloring protoplasm. Algae, plankton, freshwater kelp are either obliterated or held in blazing suspension until their chosen omnivore arrives.

The lake lies over the fault line of two tectonic plates. Temblors date back to the Pleistocene and Tertiary eras, and in the mid-nineteeth century one of them made a tsunami that flooded the settled banks, killing 1,300 fishermen and villagers. The groaning of the winds was seen by Buryats as an evil spirit that took its own sacrifices freely, drowning boat after boat of young *omul* acolytes. (The timbers of the boats were never found, the bodies annihilated.) The Evenk people's shamans also saw it as the sea-god's throne, the realm of Dianda. He, too, plucked and trimmed the tree of life, every human he wanted, from the mountaintop islands where settlements sprang up.

In autumn the curling thickets of berries blaze along the shore, and leaves lie banked on the new ice with all the colors of changing fire. From hydrofoils the lake rim looks like daubs of brilliant paint, or pellucid jellies the wind shatters and gathers together again. The leaves that make it into the water just before freezing are preserved, suspended: angels rising from the earth's god-hoard, spangles from the season's pages.

Bending over the hydrofoil rail, you can see the freshwater seals rolling and sleeping in their translucent chambers, the only freshwater seals left on earth. Their coats are black and dappled horsehide gray, or tan and

white like Guernsey cows, slate and navy and kingfisher-blue. *Nerpas*, the Buryats and Evenk call them, holy to Dianda and seldom found at their sand and wattle-hidden surface holes. By late spring they start to crowd the rocks. They live in the water's fragile illumination, and this holy light continues after death – the bodies of their dead explode in the sun, and the oil is gathered and burned in lamps in the shamans' cabins.

74

What Fits

Caregivers tried to identify each orphan with an item that would link them to the parents. For Nik'vh, and whether or not it came from the infants' actual mothers or fathers, it was a canvas belt with hooks for fishing lines and tackle. Buryat girls got seal bone barrettes, and the boys a scabbard of caribou hide trimmed in swallow feathers. Tuvan children were given cloaks or blankets in zigzag patterns, or bearing scenes of animal chases across the Altai mountain foothills.

Chukchi children were the hardest to shop for at the fabric markets. Little was known about their sparse life. Given the long nights of the Arctic, they were rumored to love vibrant-colored cloth and antler clusters, which they spun from ceiling hooks above their whale-oil lanterns. Their ways and habits were a source of mystery and few had ever even seen a Chukchi, let alone the parents of an orphan or pictures of parents.

When the first Chukchi child was two or three she took to paddling in a horse trough, arching her back in a strange butterfly stroke that seemed to come to her as naturally as walking. Someone remembered they were otter traders, and for her fourth birthday they wrapped her in an otter fur so thick and soft that a trapper, walking the halls after visiting his niece, stopped at the coat racks and stroked it as if it were the robe of a painted angel.

75

Dearth

The orphanage doctor, sitting beside me in her clogs and lab coat, is the perfect embodiment of the post-Soviet woman. The men of Russia are dying, she says. There is no one to marry here. There is no one to have children with. She squares the manila folders full of charts on her lap, looks down at them, then sets them on the chair beside her.

'It's not just here,' she says, here being Siberia, Novokuznetsk. It is even worse, she says, in Moscow, or any city in the west. The marrying kind have gotten out. All that are left are *ostatki*, the dregs, the 'ones who are the same as before' (in Soviet times): the jobless, living with their mothers, smoking in bookstores, drinking, drinking, shooting heroin and fighting, exchanging stories of how they will get out, and drinking.

Since 1989, the lifespan of the average Russian man has shortened fifteen percent, to about fifty-eight years. In Irkutsk, near Lake Baikal and squarely on the opium roads up from Afghanistan, AIDS has popped up on the menu of nightmares, almost all of it traceable to needle sharing. She tells of going there to examine a child once, how the taxi driver had to dodge the big men standing in the road, just wobbling there and tipping over.

She looks over at me. She is a true Russian beauty, with hazel eyes and slightly hennaed hair. She asks me the ages of my male friends and colleagues. A baby cries upstairs, and the slightest trace of a wince comes into her eyes. She gets up and goes.

76

Mongrel Water

The orphanage director takes me down the hall to her office as my wife tours the handicapped wing. She usually has the air of a saucy dame, a player in the sexual marketplace, but today she seems guardedly professional, even somber. She said she heard me talking about the mixture of Siberian ethnic groups.

'Why are we such mutts?' she says, pointing an accusing finger at me. 'Missionaries.' She climbs a little ladder, reaching for a multi-volume treatise. 'But not you. Most Europeans. The tsars let them in. Scottish and German.'

What she is reaching for, I see, is George Kennan (Kennan the First's) diaries of his Siberian travels. I had never touched these, but she reads English well, and I am impressed with the descriptive passages on meeting Buryat churchmen, the missionary hangers-on annoyingly in tow with Kennan. He had been ushered into a room with the head Buryat patriarch, the Khamba Lama, a Buddhist. Her finger passes slowly over the text as she reads:

'The Lama wore a striking and gorgeous costume, consisting of a superb long gown of orange silk shot through with gold thread, bordered with purple velvet, and turned back and faced at the wrists with ultra-marine blue satin ... On his head he wore a high, pointed, brimless hat of orange felt, the sides of which fell down over his shoulders.'

Kennan, she explained, went to a ceremony at the monastery's biggest temple: 'so crowded with peculiar details that one could not reduce one's observations to anything like order'. Then she describes a certain passage about the music: the chaos of flutes, drums, trumpets, gongs and vibraslaps. Then the *pièce de résistance*, which she reads with delight. Kennan had been astounded to find that the Lama had never heard of America, and thought the world was flat:

'You have been in many countries,' he said to me through an interpreter, 'and have talked with the wise men of the West; what is your opinion with regard to the shape of the earth?'

'I think,' I replied, 'that it is shaped like a great ball.'

'I have heard so before,' said the great Lama, looking

thoughtfully away into vacancy. 'The Russian officers whom I have met have told me that the world is round. Such a belief is contrary to the teachings of our old Tibetan books, but I have observed that the Russian wise men predict eclipses accurately … Why do you think the world is round?'

'I have many reasons for thinking so,' I answered. 'But perhaps the best and strongest reason is that I have been around it.'

77

Medicine

The director tells of a rumour, another sort of addiction opera, supposedly from a regional dispensary that supplies to hospitals as well as orphanages. Most missing materials can be replaced, almost immediately. But not Fentanyl, the painkiller. It is scheduled (highly monitored) by the very government that used it so disastrously in the Moscow theater hostage crisis. (Fentanyl in gas form had been pumped in by Russian state police, putting both captors and captives to sleep, slipping toward death. The antidote vans for the hostages couldn't make it through the traffic, and one hundred and twelve people died.) It is also closely watched because it is a synthetic opiate, a heroin substitute, and junkies out east in Irkutsk will pay the price of gold for it.

Two vials of the drug were missing, but no syringes.

The boxes were never checked out. The entire affair was something never meant to be seen: unseemly, pathetic, like a decaying relative who has soiled himself at a family gathering.

The director checked the pockets of coats and every departing employee's forearms. The sturdy cooks, all women over seventy, laughed at the exercise. The young stock girls rubbed their forearms warily and wiggled their mouths, looking down. The director had to check everyone, every single employee be they full-time, part-time or independent. The last one she checked was the dispensary doctor. Surely, for all this woman has told me, it could not have been her. Every life within her ambit is like a candle, a little egg she races on the end of a spoon and that she must never, but never, let drop.

78

Two-sided Picture

The orphanage doctor was again in despair of the husband situation. The babies reminded her, of course, of this sole remaining gap in her life. She referred to it as a *pustota*, a 'void'.

Which led to more lectures on the Russian man, the Russian male character, its appalling absence. She ran her finger along the right angles of one of her case folders, counterposing human vacillation with the certainties of geometry.

'The Russian man has no honor,' she said. 'He is like the sailor man in the movie *Captain*.'

I drew a blank.

'You know?' she asked.

I was thinking of Humphrey Bogart in *To Have And Have Not*.

'Alec Guinness,' she said. 'He has wife in Gibraltar. Mistress in Tangier.'

Wavelets of grey came into my mind. White puffs from a steamer swaying under the great rock.

'He has picture,' she said, resting the file vertically like a portrait on her knees. 'On one side his wife, other side the mistress.'

She looked out the window. 'When wife riding with him, her picture. When is night, mistress riding? He take picture down and turn it over.'

She didn't reverse the file, but her finger flicked the backside with a crack. A cloud of dust came up.

The notes on the tab of the file had only the mother's name. If the father in the case were known, it would be written right under hers. 'Your baby's mother's name here on yours, father's name just below. Most of them like this. No father's name.'

She lays the files down and picks up the Marlboros, knocking them against her closed fist before opening the cellophane. I pull the matches out of my pocket.

79

Duck Rabbit

When you signal to a baby, you see there is no meaning in the sign itself. One wants to say the sign *contains* its meaning, or that the baby feels compelled to follow the sign in a certain way. It goes back to Wittgenstein's problem of the sideways pointing finger. How do I know my observer doesn't see the direction I'm trying to create as indicated by the crook my thumb and finger make, rather than the tip of my finger?

Amelia is on the other side of the room, having just finished playing with her ball. I want her to come to me, and raise my voice sweetly, to what I imagine to be an entreating tone. *Come here.* She does nothing.

I raise my hands, palms facing me, and gesture toward my face with both sets of fingers. *Come here*, it says. It *has* to say.

But she tries to raise both hands like I did. This she cannot do yet. Can her interpretation be only to imitate?

I take my hands and make the 'come here' gesture I have seen in other cultures, in Mexico, here in Russia, etc., which is just to pat the ground with one's palms.

She looks at me for a minute. She puts her hands down as if to start crawling in my direction.

But I see that she smiles, and she's finished. She stays put. She, too, pats the ground, twice, three times with her tiny palms.

80

The Unadopted

The second floor of the orphanage contains the cold, consistent stuff of heartbreak. We were told we would not be brought up here, but the director in her zeal wants to show off the 'adaptations' that have been made. We go past the tiny but brightly polished wing for Down's Syndrome children, babies through pre-adolescence, the oldest probably twelve or thirteen. Most lay on the floor on mats, but all are tended to. Unlike the rest of the place, where there are eight to ten caretakers per child, each disabled child has an adult tender.

The chance of a child being adopted past three or four begins to evaporate, declining to almost zero by the teenage years. With any disability those odds are multiplied by ten, perhaps a hundred. What to think of the couples we met on the plane who take the most retarded and enfeebled? Usually they have an agenda. Almost invariably they are Pentecostals, with a muted but highly charged blueprint for soul-saving – the dry drunks of the world of messianic religions. But the net effect of their efforts is to get these kids out of here. You want to embrace these religionists. The word 'good' was made to apply to them. Their deeds are Yeats's heavenly mansion, raging in the dark.

We are brought into a television room, kids of all stripes sitting in front of Barney. They have been trained not to look at visitors, to keep their eyes on the tube. We stand behind them awkwardly, watching Baby Bop dancing in his giant yellow tennis shoes.

When we begin to leave it is the ones with rolling eyes and sloped faces that ignore their training and come toward us. The rest simply rise and show their manners, saying '*Po-ka, po-ka*' (an informal goodbye). The challenged children lurch forward, escaping the grip of their watches, saying 'Mama … Papa.'

81

Baby A.

For a year, all she has seen is stuffed animals, drawings of animals, fluffy bears and wolves held up above her crib by storytellers. At the Kemerovo restaurant – Traktor, it is called, and truly *is* a crossroads here – a young, beautiful Tartar girl wants to take Amelia from me and march her over to her boyfriend and his pals. The girl is ecstatic, crying '*Krasivaya, krasivaya*' (beautiful) as I follow her through the crowd.

Amelia, too new to all of this to be upset, sees just another caretaker, albeit inside a whirlpool of lights and noise, all red, red, red, like the Matisse in the Hermitage with the vine winding toward the frumpy woman and her set table.

I should have known I was in for it when we reach the man-tent. Boyfriend and mates are very drunk, four empty bottles of Imperia on the table, one tipped on its side. A thick white curtain of Marlboro smoke. She introduces me to all of them and he is cordial but taken aback when girlfriend puts my daughter in his face.

'*Vot*,' she says; I want one of these. His mates laugh at him, *the reaper is nigh*, and he lifts both hands in a slow-down, steady everything movement. Girlfriend squeals out something and shakes Amelia from side to side gently, like a rag doll.

She is given back to me and smiles as I put the top of her head to my nose. My wife wondering where we are, I see her waving from the distance in the other dining room.

Then, in the doorway, Amelia sees it: a real dog, somewhat of a rare sight in modern Russia, which tends to be cat country. It is some kind of terrier. Larger, maybe a sheltie. I point to its uplifted nose, taking in the waft of food smells that have to be a kind of dog paradise. She's fixed on him. He yaps. She is fearless, waiting to see if he'll go away, bark again, or turn into something else.

82

Yellowing

Morning in the orphanage. Great columns of sun filled with motes of dust, yellow in the yellow light, and clumps of it the same color as they gather in the corners and on the stairs. 'Good morning Mr Sun' was my first song, and George Harrison's 'Here Comes The ...' the first tune I could get the twins to pay attention to on the car stereo. My earliest memory in the dark, satanic, Presbyterian church Sunday school, under the rafters of its whale-ribbed nave: Miss Chipps leading us through 'Jesus Wants Me For A Sunbeam'.

Zhol-ty, Zhol-ty in Russian. Similar in German.

A divine color, the color of butter and good fortune and blessings, of graduation tassles and Hindu marigolds. Goan and Parati houses – bright saffron with white-trimmed doorjambs and windowsills and shutters. Yellow the color of the blanket we first saw Amelia in, spread like a king's robe on the doctor's palm where she was perched.

83

Id River

Orphanage children are put on toilets as soon as they can sit. Pots, literally, not the plastic baby contraptions you see in the West, but discarded, blackened kitchen pots which shed soft ash.

They wave to us as we pass the long toilet-and-shower complex, just as the kids watching TV had. One of them tries to get up, but the *matas* here are particularly harsh and a single look sends the girl back down.

'Love hath pitched his mansion in the place of excrement.' First the children are taught to self-soothe – their cries after lights out are simply ignored. The stern, early, consistent toilet training is the second of things that shock us. There are stories of adoptees later shrieking at the sight of anything resembling what they are planted on now.

What to hold back and what to extrude are our first claims of command over the world, and those who shape our manner of commanding shape everything else. We begin by irrupting ourselves, pouring the urgent and pure, unmediated voice out into the dark. No one answers, no one comes. The circle of cold steel circumscribes our bums.

84

Knowing

Amelia is beginning to take advantage. She knows if she cries loud enough, we will come. My wife is better at letting her cry now than I am.

How to tell what she is thinking? She never took the breast. Does that mean she will never have the idealized *imago* the object-relations theorists talk about? Is her idealization formed with whoever will hold her, whether or not it then gives her food?

Are her mental events confined only to food and discomfort (warmth, cold)? Is there something more complex beneath the blue, blinking pools? Is there at least fear, euphoria, serenity? Is love at this stage based on trust, dependency, consistency?

She's like an ice fairy, a sprite, unreadable. But she knows, or reacts with something like knowledge, that everything is changed now. Send out a cry and something will come.

85

Eves of the New Wings

Some of the young orphanage workers are radiant *devushki*. They dress much more skankily than even the complaining, husband-trolling doctors. Miniskirts, fishnet stockings, heels and boots so narrow they seem designed to break the bones. Eye make-up is heavy, lurid, 'tarty' to the Irish mothers here to pick up their white-haired choices.

They are coquettish, laying long gazes on almost any young man, whether or not in tow of a wife. Out east of here, in Irkutsk, where the factories are closing, they are pushers and call girls. The channels of livelihood are choking, withering away. They walk the brown, rocky streets looking for johns. What the Ukrainian pimps don't take they spend on the *manna* Afghanistan sends up, the poisoned gift bestowed on Russia for invading.

Here, where dope is less easy to come by, they find oblivion in the same clear liquid they claim has taken the men. In the mornings, some of the mop girls totter. Then comes the door of the toilet shutting, and then the retching.

86

The Hordes,
Last Glimpses of

The valleys just south of the orphanage are in the Gorno-Altaisk, close to the even wilder and further valleys where the frontiers of China, Kazakhstan, Russia and Mongolia come together. It is a vast stage containing an ancient, holy and intrepid mixture of people. Some are Mongol-Turkic tribesmen, semi-nomadic people whose ancestors came with the armies of Genghis Khan.

The Altai and Sayan mountains separate Siberia from the Central Asian steppes proper. Its people are Mongol-featured even though they call themselves Caucasians. In the city, they have been pushed aside by the European Russians of the Northwest. The Altai's people live in the cracks and margins, a life of being 'on the Rez' much like displaced Native Americans. They work as custodians

and road laborers, cooks and waiters and, if they are lucky, merchants and salespeople.

They have faces of immediately appreciable character, tawny and narrow-eyed, but with fairer-colored and smoother skin that has escaped the harshness of the steppe winds. Much of their expressive power seems held in a grimace, but it is simply the way they smile.

And yet for all their travails, they are resented by the whites. A boorish civil servant told me that is was his people – Soviet people – who gave the Altais all they have ever had. When pressed, the 'education' he speaks of is really just Communist Party history, Dialectical Materialism I, II, III and so on. The Altais were always kept out of the social services, just as Peter the Great kept them out of his.

But preferences have been recently established for them, and this perceived 'reverse discrimination' is what sets my speaker off.

The man chews and spits sunflower seeds, lifting his half-closed, slobbery palm to his mouth. 'Now they have the inside track. My kids have to score higher, or leave town to go to another city's school.' He fishes a shell from a pile of teeth that look like shattered sewer tiles. 'They come into the village to drink. Have no words with them. They cannot manage their alcohol.'

His error is obvious from the fact that they run the orphanage kitchens. No kindness can be added to their kindness. Their custom is to fleck the dullest starches and breads with something ambrosial: milk with cumin and honey, ginger in the meat. Under the teapot top two long, brown sprigs of buffalo grass.

87

Nut Bus Driver

Aside from the orphanage itself, the orphanage town is best known for being the home of the Nut Bus Driver. About ten years before, the Nut Bus Driver, after stopping at a roadside bar for some illegal vodka, came out to find that the fifty-odd mental patients he had been transporting from Novosibirsk to Omsk had escaped.

They had escaped quickly, as they were unchained, unrestrained, not on any medication. He looked carefully to all sides of the horizon but they had either made it through the steppe grass or were hiding in a ditch or culvert somewhere, waiting for him to give up and drive off.

Not wanting to admit his mistake, he drove to an actual bus stop on the country highway and asked the forty-odd passengers waiting on the benches if they wanted a free ride to Omsk. They assented and boarded the bus.

There were no records at the departure hospital, the receiving hospital, or on the bus itself of who had been selected for relocation.

When the driver arrived in Omsk with his passengers, he told the attending physician that the group was indeed profoundly insane, affected by the particular disorder of thinking themselves sane and being unable to be talked out of it. They were terribly effective at this, having long periods of lucidity or possessing such fugue states of silent, normal-seeming decorum that no staff could ever suspect their true instability.

The mistake went undetected for three days, when the new inmates made a racket against the ward doors with their metal cups. The driver was finally apprehended and himself committed.

88

River Ghost

Being near the rivers, the orphanage always had an abundance of Caspian sturgeon. This was the fish whose meat had been sought by kings for centuries, and in fact had been declared as owned – every one of them in every water body – by the Tsar under royal decree.

Proximity would have spoiled the cooks of another establishment. But here it was never treated as just another fish, it was loved intensely and never taken for granted. The older children ate filets, and the babies had it chopped almost into purées, or mixed with milk into a kind of stew.

We would see them delivered whole. The precious roe eggs had been stripped out of them, tiny red or oily black marbles scooped into coolers and flown to four-star hotels in Rostov and Moscow. The carcasses dripped

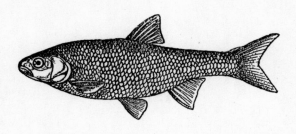

with river water, their own secretions, hazel disinfectants. The whiskered heads swayed back and forth like sleeping bats.

Out in the river, the sturgeon was falling asleep. She had no self-consciousness, but noticed the hot and cold and in-between temperatures of the currents, the day's light lowering, the rising dust and silt of falling stones. She bent herself into a coil, winding several times till her snout touched her tail like Ourobouros, her whiskers buried in the warmer silt, the deep enchanted stuff that held the whole day's sun. Her tendrils ruffled in the passing water, her eyes open as she drifted toward sleep. Her scales lifted in rapid, cold, padded sheets, fluttering and flattening. The apparatus of pincers and feelers was guided by great round eyes, lightless because of her shallow station, the tendrils whirling wildly like some anti-halo of Leviathan.

She slept. The current could not lift her from her rock. She could not hear the net men coming, the rubber hammers of their moving boots.

89

Food: A Prosecutor's Story

I am a prosecutor for the Russian Federation, Oblast of Kemerovo. I prosecute adoptions, principally. 'Prosecution' is not exactly the right word, the right concept for a prosecutor's role in an adoption. It is mainly a review, a process whereby we inspect the parents. They have their own lawyers if something goes wrong, if papers are missing or the court file is incomplete. But things are almost always in order.

I am happy to give these children to the American couples, because many come to us malnourished. By recommending to the Judge that the state has no objection to the adoptive parents, I am doing many things: giving children a future, an education, a ticket to a more stable world.

But first I am giving them food, sustenance. When I contemplate my work, that is the stuff I think and dream of most.

Whenever we children wouldn't eat something our mother had cooked, my father told us one of his starvation stories, usually the one about the Magadan camp children and their tiny, gold-covered chocolate coin. The children were being singled out and punished for something, and had been without food for a good four or five days. The coin had dropped from the pocket of the guard who had come to check up on them. They were lucky it was wrapped in gold foil. Almost any other type of food – a bit of bread or dried meat, for example – wouldn't even have been found. It would have been invisible, he said, in the light of the one weak lamp that hung above the barracks.

There were so many children that they had to share (sharing was another of the story's lessons). They lined up one by one, peeled back the delicate wrapper, and wet a finger, circling the coin's edges in turn until each one had just enough to put a taste on their tongue. My youngest sister Lena would stop swinging her feet at this, looking down somberly and twisting her fork. My mother's eyes brimmed reverently with tears. I would listen too, but also seized the moment to slip my offending portion under the table to our dog, whose enormous, undiscriminating jaws would start their noiseless lapping across the giant plate.

I didn't mean by this to dismiss my father; the lesson of the tale was true enough, and I would feel more than a little guilt at what I was doing. In fact, as his voice rose, deathly quiet, almost whispering through his description of the ragged, dusty band of them, their images rose before me, even more real than the three attentive women surrounding me at the table. And the dog's warm, rapid, grainy tongue on my fingers – the feel, it seemed, of hunger itself – would also help to make vivid the children's hair and hollow eyes, and their own much thinner and bonier fingers, slowly circling the tiny, opened petal of foil.

The essence of hunting, Ortega y Gasset tells us, is that the animal, the game, the *food* we are seeking, is elusive, has a chance to get away. (It is what another writer tells us makes bullfighting both interesting and fair.) This might explain, if anything can, the hunting passion around which my father and his brothers seemed to shape their lives in those years. As all of them settled into relatively stable lives, Party membership and certain money, something instinctual was missed: the seeking and finding, the chasing of what could be lost or missed altogether. Food as something that had to be gone after, *worked for*.

And for the food, or what could become the food, to itself *fight back*. That was taking the concept further, and I knew this from reading my father's hunting magazines. Black bears had killed men on the same Ob River trails he hunted every year; and caribou could lunge, their antlers a rack of dull blades, at the stalker who sneaked up on them too quickly. But none of the animals seemed to come back at him like this. They acquiesced, as peaceful and pliant as the trout I pulled with him into our fishing boat.

And yet there was one prey that fought, and it was when I was with my father, and it was fish. They were pike, with jaws and teeth as sharp and narrow as a dog's.

They fought him all the way up into the boat on a trolling spoon, and once inside the thwarts, I had to gaff them for long, horrible minutes until they died, showering us with blood and scales and sometimes the hooks of the lure they had flung from their gills. They fought so hard I could never really believe they were dead. My father put them on the stringer while I rested, the rusted bar slippery with gore where it rested between my legs.

The peace, the comfort of having the game in hand: I felt it, too, beneath the gruesomeness of what we were doing when we cleaned his squirrels and rabbits, the white fur bellies opening under the *militsa* knife and the purple bag of guts bulging out in a pod, and the blood dripping, dripping down on the spread newspaper, on the pictures of running footballers, and the smiling, waving young American president.

90

Food: A Prosecutor's Story II

The images become indelible as I watch new coverage of the famine and warfare in the Sudan. The images clutch around my heart like dread, like the little prongs that hold a diamond solitaire. It is hard to tell the dying from the dead. The TV camera rests on a stooped body, and you keep waiting for it to move. Then, finally, you see something like a fly lighting on the eye, and you wonder if it had taken the cameraman as long as it took you to realize what was going on. Day after day we see them walk, carrying their bowls across the blowing roads. The desert has moved in on them, a foot or two a month. It chokes their plows. The factions – three of them – position themselves each morning along the changing configurations of the desert.

Most war is about land, and most land is about food and the power or the faith it nourishes. The leaders of the factions and relief workers stood guard over the grain sacks throughout Darfur, and in the crumbling warehouses of the far interior. But the work of the guards is impossible. Who is more fearless than the starving and dying? They pulse outward from the famined back country – Rismayo and Merca and Baidoa – in Somalia, India, Bangladesh, Rwanda, wherever hunger looms now as a menace – floating like spores, like sniffing rats, to raid the rows of sacks that were meant, eventually and in some small measure, for themselves and their fellow villagers. If they only knew it, all they would have to do is wait, because the sentry is paid too little; too little is put in his bowl, too. He weakens and topples with sleep before they can even take out their knives. They grab his gun and drag him away to be shot. (Care must be taken, bullets can puncture the burlap.) They return to the sack piles, put a man on each corner, nimble as jewel thieves unlatching glass cases of gems.

States of privation, of *de*privation. We see them everywhere once we're out in the grocery store parking lots; rags and bottles of water in their hands, shopping carts, children and cardboard signs: 'Chechnya Veteran' and 'Need Work'. Scores of them rush at me from the factory entrances at twilight, clothes flapping in the wind. Once I am out of change the last of them flits through the hole in the cyclone fence and down to the darkening mounds of the construction site.

The eyes here have grown hollower, for there are a few that we recognize. And no matter how many there are and how closely they crowd together, we never for a second confuse any two of them. The crowd of faces never merges. These are not the masses our distance makes of the dead at Ingushetia or their neighboring cities, the 'mountain phantoms'. These stay differentiated. Pain and hunger individualize. However much a face might thin and tend toward the skull, the stamp of its self shines out like a weakening lamp. It is this, this light, that makes us feel their pain, feel ourselves in their shoes.

Food as a paradise of flavor and abundance, a Garden of Earthly Delights. It is this heaven, this brimming Eden the hungry are cast from. They want a return to the furnishings of the fallen world just like we want a return to that first world, where we didn't even have the knowledge of want. There are places where food, or the raw stuff of whatever will become it, comes at us with a richness we see nowhere else. And that richness becomes the place, becomes what it is.

I think of Tomsk on winter mornings as a girl, rubbing my hands at my cook stall by the brick paprika factory. Its chimney belched like a tiny old pipe-smoking man, and its red dust covered everything. Even the landscape seemed to be waiting those few seconds for one of the

Hungarian pastries the wife of the owner cooked, the grains of paprika settling down on the snow, on the black slapping wipers and the yellow hood, and in my hair. The old woman pulled the pastry from the oven and put it on wax paper, and I smelled another puff from the chimney, and just as the hot iced (and now grainy) bun touched my fingers I would think how the name of the thing – the burst of the 'p' and the long vowels – embodied its wonderful cloudiness, and I would sometimes even say it to myself: *Paprika, paprika, paprika*, standing there as the light came into the street.

Or Singapore, where my mother worked in the embassy and I got visas to visit her. The racks of peppers and yams and ginseng never dried from the wet that hung in the air all day as you walked, as the vendors chattered and their tiny Hindu cymbals crashed. Fish, flesh and fowl hung from the strings, glazed and dripping with some kind of sugared marmalade. Whole sides of beef hung down, fat brahmas from Johore Bahru, whose meat was cut in tiny strips covered with gnats or split in two, their centers soaking with seeds and slush. Flours and powders and grains in little beveled cones with terraced, checkered siding, dried buds in bowls of frangipani water.

And all of it led, the whole churning tunnel, down through the dripping public garden, along the path they called the tiger walk, for the last live wild tiger seen on the streets of Singapore. He walked the entire length of

Bencoolen Road, hungry as he was, and shooed away by nervous, muttering vendors, walked up the steps of the Raffles Hotel, where they shot him under a snooker table chewing one of the bartender's bloody hands.

So much of a country is found in its dishes, what the population yearns for and how badly. Supper is the last common ritual we celebrate before sleep, our reward for being drained and laden: the crown of the day.

There is no heaven back here in Kemerovo now, no bounty by the empty produce stalls in Koreatown where I wait for the guard to open the courthouse door. I will go in a few minutes to buy my donuts and coffee before going upstairs to prepare my argument. I'll pass the same number of open hands between here and there: the man I see now running his fingers across the lettuce rack, a woman with a pram covered by water-beaded plastic, a little girl selling her pink 'I Am Deaf' cards with their solemn, silent rows of hand speech.

Usually there are more here than the few I see gathered this morning. Usually, almost always, hordes of them circle the stall and trade off with each other, bending and grabbing the brown-patched outer leaves of the lettuce the ladies pick off and throw in the barrels. Once they have their pieces they sit on the narrow berms of the car spaces, bent over like Daumier's angels in Hades. Then they bite down carefully and begin to chew, and with each motion of their mouths they look more like angels.

This is a splendid modern courthouse, and the elevators pass at every floor great square windows that show the market lot and the grabbing angel gaggle of lettuce-eaters. Every lunch now we eat Chinese, and I'm going to take some of what's left today out to the parking lot. As we rise I look out; I feel guilty about what seems to be my own small, selfish hunger, guilty about the food that I've bought. I can feel the cold air in the shafts as I tear off pieces of donut and taste the sugar and dough on my tongue. And outside now in the lot I can see the circle of my father and the camp children gathered under the barracks lamp, and imagine the sweet, dark drops on their hands.

91

Tyumen Is
My Dwelling Place

There was another incident with my Uncle Dmitri. As before, it involved his trying to come for Sunday supper, and my mother keeping him from coming inside, and his waiting for some time before getting back in his car and driving back to Moscow again. These times are painful, but they are a test of us. *Lo are the tested the true vine*, it is written; *only the tempest of wickedness sures the binding of its troth*.

We live in the city of Tyumen here in the most removed and earliest-settled places east of the Urals. The great main river of the same name flows through here, and each of its five branches flow through each of the five adjoining towns and out into the Obskaya Gulf. All the rivers' names come from the native Siberian tribes, who we learned from Patriarch Yoshkar were the very sons of the original Tribes of Cain. Their languages were beautiful, he said, but their savagery caused them to turn aside the olive branch of our forefathers, the White Russian settlers, and lose forever the chance of redemption our ancestors offered them.

We ourselves are Orthodox, from the Eastern Church in what was once Byzantium. We believe the Scriptures are the actual and unmediated Word of God. We believe it is the Truth of His mouth as He has chosen to constitute and deliver it through the earthly vessels of His Prophets. We believe he has *lifted all veils*, and where he has not has *fitted the figure of nature to make his Revelations plain*.

I am eighteen, the last of three girls. There are twelve of us living here in our three houses, but I am the only one of this age: too old for school but too young to leave home yet, waiting to see which way in the world I am pointed to go. I have two sisters with husbands and children still in the earlier grades. I was born late. A *gift*, my father said. Dmitri is my mother's only sibling, the only brother. My father was an only child, so Dmitri is in fact the only relation we have inside that generation.

My father is an old-style Soviet father, a stonemason, a valuable trade. Without him and those of his craft, there would be no building, *no dwelling rising up from the waste of the plain*. He is a tall man, his arms large with the strength of his building. His eyes are flat and gray as the mortar he cleaves the stones with, and though he smiles, the corners of his mouth turn down at the same time, strangely, with the steady tap and scrape and wiping trowel of his authority. It is happiness like the Lord's own happiness, a joy that is filled with the work ahead and hence will have no truck with nonsense. It is happiness, but a happiness without laughter.

My mother is a cripple. Even so, her nature is more gay than his. She walks with one crutch only. She does not lean on it but swings it around and pulls herself forward to the place where she has planted it. Her eyes are blue, bright blue as bellflowers, and her hair is yellow-bright as the corn that has withered young and will never harden and change.

She takes the edge off his cold steel, she says, and this is the way things are on the day of Dmitri's visits.

For hours before Dmitri comes, my father goes on and on about Moscow. Moscow is Sodom, he says. It is a City of the Plain as festering as the cities written of in the accounts of the prophets. No good grows there, he will mutter. He says it from under the *Pravda* that's open in front of his face.

Mother's eyes look at mine as we work, bright bellflower blue, and I want her to sometimes raise them at me in some kind of small complicity. But this she will not do. She looks down when her eyes meet mine and she shakes her head. The problem of Dmitri is hardest by far for her, as he is the baby brother she mothered as much as her own mother did, and sees now in her later years what has come of that, of raising him up among an absence of men.

It will take Dmitri a good thirteen hours to drive here. It would only be half a day on a good road, but the roads to these back places are unpaved and potted, and some still have one-lane bridges over the five rivers.

I see him setting out from his apartment – a townhouse, it is called – right now, after walking his tiny dog and setting the alarm with the keypad on the wall. Dmitri is always well-groomed, like all of his friends, all men. He is clean and good-smelling, bright as a *kopeck*. I watched him lock the door like this once and when he put the key in his pocket I could see the heavy ID bracelet fall down and glint on his wrist.

Dmitri has neighbors in Moscow. *His* neighbors. All young men and professors like him, and students. They seem happy, full of their music and learning. What is that if not fraternity? It is *their* fraternity. They laugh loudly, shaking the ice in their drinks and mock-punching one another. Some even go to church. To churches filled with others like them, men linked together with other men.

My father and my brothers-in-law argue about the mason guilds and scripture in the same conversation. This is how our faith is lived, I've heard him say. There is no separation of the supernatural from the natural.

When I am at Dmitri's, the world here feels like it is the opposite of him. Opposed and parallel, like Dr Klebem says in chemistry class, the magnets whipping each other away from their force fields, gathering the flower shapes of the iron filings around themselves. I believe that I would flourish there, in Moscow, like a rose in the meadow grasses. My faith would not falter but would give me strength, the very strength that everyone here is constantly talking about.

It would be as if I lived in another country. I could live, I know, among other people as certainly as I live here now, even if I did not know their language. I see myself in a restaurant, running my finger down the lines of the menu with my eyes closed. At the instant I open them I say a passage out of Corinthians, and where my finger has stopped I will know the words.

My sister Sveta is staring at me. Her face is plain, like the women in photographs of the Great Patriotic War, with all their beauty and desire burned away and bleached down into a brown monotone. But she loves me. This I know. I see it in the steadiness of her hands tossing up the cut tips of the blood-red peppers and vegetables.

She, like Irina, who is two years her elder, is the true breadwinner of her family. Sveta works full time as the church secretary. Her husband Zeb, or Zebulon, preserves old threshing machines and tractors for the farmers here.

But it is not a steady occupation, and vodka has been known to take him away for a time.

My father passes food to Zeb, who passes it to Irina and her husband Georgi. Father and Georgi agree that Solzhenitsyn is a huckster and embodies the worst traits of evangelism. When they tell jokes about the great writer, my father makes the kind of smile of which he is capable, the expression that is grimacing and lean.

I hear the wheels of Dmitri's car in the driveway.

The sound of the door of a car like his is soft, a cluck, like someone clucking his tongue in their mouth. His steps are a long time on the gravel, tiny crunches in the stones, and then they are on the boards of the porch.

My father raises his hand in the half-second before the knock, as though he could tell the precise instant when it would come. My mother gets up, the beginnings of a flash of defiance on her face. But she knows even as she is making it that she will not cross him. She walks not to the door, even though there is a second knock, but to the oven, where something that is baking needs to be tended to.

Under the cover of her movements, I can lean back and see him through the blinds, standing and shifting with his hands in his pockets. I cannot see his head. He is wearing khaki pants and a tight, form-fitting maroon sweater under his black leather coat. The ID bracelet glimmers in the sun, hanging heavy on his graceful wrist.

'Leave it,' says father. He is talking about the cake and Dmitri both. My mother paces back and forth now in the shaft of sunlight.

'Leave it,' my father says again. His hand is still hanging in the air. 'Don't answer.'

The burning feeling has spread to the tips of my fingers and toes and into my hair now, it seems. I imagine it in the hollows of my bones. It is the power, I imagine, that some mothers have when they are able to lift cars up off their children. *What strengths come from a righteous fury. What lay upon the face of the earth hath traveled, even unto its darkling core.*

Dmitri has never knocked a third time. He has once or twice walked to a window whose blinds are bent enough for him to think he can see in, but nothing is seen by either him or us. This time he does nothing. He walks back to the car, through the gravel noises and the door's cluck and the sudden awakening of the expensive engine's hum, everything reversing.

Not long ago I had a dream of Dmitri. We were looking at one another through a great porch screen. It was either the big one that wraps around the Moscow apartment or the one right here, the one he knocked on today and that stands not four feet from me now as I write this.

The barrier it amounts to had begun to dissolve. It faded and blended with the sky behind it so that our hands could pass to one another's. My fingers kept going past his open palm, reaching in between his ribs as I imagine God's hand had reached into Adam's.

For a moment, joined together as we were, I felt as though I had come to a place prepared for us like the banquet table in the psalm, a place of shelter in the presence of our enemies. A made place, a place of first permission. We could be there *spirit to spirit, as one spirit* and as we had been in the briefness of the moments at his house parties, or when our eyes would meet across the sea of heads in the cool dark of Belorussia Station. *Spirit to spirit. Bright center of heaven.*

But it is only a dream, and I knew as the power drained out of me that it had to remain such. To hear the knock is glorious. To hear the knock could be one's heart's desire. But to open the door and actually go out. That is something different. That is something else entirely.

92

Belo

One doctor could not stand the whiteness surrounding him. From the office window he watched the drifts swirl up over the fence tops, nestled like starched collars around the tall-necked spruces.

The wind blew them into patterns, no two alike. Long sheets sparkled and flattened, growing knobs and hollows when the breezes changed direction. Most twisted into simple juggernauts, innocent as the soft ice creams of his childhood summers. Others were menacing: concave faces collapsing immensely forward, the underlying pasture grasses sharpened to brows and noses – a scattered Easter Island of the sub-zero.

But all of it was white, as white as his newly starched lab coat. It suffocated him. No variation could offset the terrifying sameness. He felt unmoored at times. He felt like he imagined the Yakut shamans to be, without any system of measurement save for the passage of time. Five days through the whiteness was fifty kilometers, ten days was one hundred.

A child had left a kaleidoscope behind in one of the examining rooms. The doctor carried it in the pocket of his lab coat. Sitting down at the window, he knew he didn't even need to turn it to behold luxuriance. The shattered pile of summer colors prodded his senses awake again. Sheets upon sheets lay there for his assembly, like the hardened shards of oils on a painter's floor.

He twisted the tube: a star, a flower, a compass dial or a rim of spidery silver nets. The chips slipped in and out of one another like little molecular engines, creating anything and nothing at once. Its designer must have known of the Solid Mandala, the earth's core to certain aboriginal (and then Hindu and Buddhist) sects, nothing more than the Sanskrit *mandalam,* for 'circle' or 'periphery'. The entirety of its plane was evenly colored, center and rims, energy charging out and splashing back, the confining circumference.

The tube made a whooshing sound as he turned it, not unlike the sea sound of a conch's shell. The life of color was his at last, growing out of the bone hues of absence and oblivion. He started to catalogue the shapes as he would the flora of an undiscovered island. He remembered the Dutch sailor marooned in the South Seas, charting new taxonomies of plants as his eyesight faded. These snows the doctor planted his shapes upon may as well have been the same blackness the sailor battled. Indeed, when the doctor closed his eyes it was the patterns he saw now, vivid bursts on the ink of the void.

It became his church, his faith, his regulating and defining habit. It was what he imagined the poor medieval serfs must have made of cathedrals' stained glass windows: God's fire and ever-sparking embers, carrying holiness and peace. He remembered what the sailor said to the men who found him, laying back on the beach with his vision gone: 'It is all alive here in the darkness.'

93

Soldier of the Caucasus

I ran across a young colonel who had commanded troops in the Caucasus. He and his friend were weaving around the club car of the Novsibirsk-Irkutsk express, bringing back pints of Altai beer, grabbing the waitress who came to clean up after them, pleading with the kitchen to stay open later. He was young for a colonel, but was my age (forty-nine). During the seventies, the Soviet presence in Egypt was such that he was in and out of Alexandria and points west with great frequency, including Libya and Algeria, then strongly aligned with the USSR, and Morocco, which was neutral. All the soldiers smoked *kif* when they could get it. He told me of this episode, which he said scared him as much as anything he had seen twenty years later in Grozny:

We bought the *kif* from a Moroccan kid – probably

a soldier – on the Tripoli-Rabat express, handing over the quartered *dinar* notes for the four or five flat-rolled *zagarettes*, clipped and trim and even. We stood facing him, holding onto what we could, hand straps and seats and backpacks, rocking, swaying as we raced down through the date oases at the desert's edges. We got it not so much for wanting it as for the bad way the kid had taken Radetsky's joke – *Nous sommes Algerien* – which made him frown and look as if he were reaching in his *djellabah* for something harmful. So we bought it out of shame, as a sort of apology. We hadn't known how much the Algerians were hated, how fierce the battle had become with them for the Spanish Sahara.

Radetsky, whose instincts I would later stake my life on, had said the wrong thing, the wise thing, the thing that could get your throat cut. So we were forced into being supplicants, which in the Third World meant that most essential sort of other humans: consumers, customers.

Radetsky was red-faced, downcast as the strong-chested boy stuffed the bills in the pocket of his gray striped robe. *Jieux, joux*, said my companion, searching for the word 'joke'. *Les jeux sont faits*, said the Moroccan soldier: the game is up.

The whistle blew. The stop was a garrison of the militia, and he got off.

The stops increased. More and more people got off the train, and the clusters of buildings thickened. I got

212

out of my rucksack the books the Petersburg editor had given me, and which I was supposed to bring back for the magazine and translate: Yacoubi and Mohammed Mrabet, books whose loose, soft phrasing could build up your Maghrebi if you digested a line or two a day. Badi, my tutor, would ride the train with us from Fez to Tangier in order to correct my selections, not only in Arabic, but in Dinka and Pygmy languages as well.

Our hotel room looked out over the *mamounia*, the old tanneries whose stink was legendary: a hellish, rancid stench that gave you tears and jagged fits of coughing. But it also masked any odor one brought to the room. So after dinner that night Radetsky opened a book of mine and took out one of the sticks. As he lit it I could see its oval circumference, and as he passed it to me the brays of the donkeys pulling the tanning buckets grew louder.

The *kif* was ravishing. My spine felt lined with something like a ridge of tongues, and honey poured along them, cooling and pulsing, cooling and pulsing like the morphine wash they had given me once for kidney stones. The sounds of the prayer callers had started and mixed with the donkey's brays and creaking of the wood and ropes. It was the 'violet hour', the time the long day's haze made all the buildings' edges wash and seep up toward the giant, starless night.

There was a knock on the door. Before the slowed-down sound of it ended the knocker had opened it, and

Radetsky made a sudden gesture toward the window, pointing, violently pushing.

'Control,' said the man who had entered. Behind him there was another man. The speaking man had large, scratched glasses and an open shirt. The one behind him had a narrow, sweating face, and his cotton *dhoura* was buttoned to the top. The first man made a sniffing sound.

'Control?' Radetsky asked, his left eye cocked.

I watched the streams of sweat on the main man's neck. His hand was open in the air, a plastine picture on the right and crooked typing on the facing side. No badge. No gun. But he was real.

Radetsky asked again. My heart pressed up against the sides of my ribs, like some sort of swelling fruit.

'Do you want to see …?' The man's voice trailed off, and he made a clasping motion with one hand over the wrist of the other.

Radetsky shook his head, and I saw now it was a sort of cooperation, a disarming honesty he was going for. Something incredulous and Russian. He bunched his mouth to say: no disbelief, no disrespect intended.

Main man's eyes and nose followed the trail of scent out onto the roof. My heart was like a rabbit now. The seconds were long, dull flashes of panic. Looking at Radestsky's hands, making sure they were open, I thought of my first near bust in the relative comfort of my own country.

Mounted police had come down to a circle of us in Gorky Park, their horses stamping and chafing as one of them dismounted. We'd thrown the joint away, but their hands went through our shirt pockets until they found the film canister in Sergei's. He was the one they took in. But we knew where to find him, and when, and how to go about it. They wrote him a ticket for 'hooliganism'. There were no surprises inside the surprise.

Not having found anything, the men came and sat down on the desk chairs. They were ready to negotiate, for all I knew, on matters they had yet to propose – an offer waiting in a place they would haul us down to or had prepared in the room next to ours. I could imagine paying all the money we had left to them. Or worse: I saw myself locked away, outside the reach of diplomatic help, my twenties evaporating into something I'd know later only as static time – a thing I'd never lived, a droplet I had never tasted.

But the two of them were winded from the search on the roof. They struck us now, with their heavy breathing and heaving, sodden shirts, as cops too young to pull off a plant, rookies too green for crookedness.

When they left Radetsky and I looked at one another, not speaking, reeling out the fear we could sense in each other. After a minute or two I could see his fingers shaking, a true tremor, like an old man with a disease.

At first I thought Radetsky was watching the spasms

of his hands, which he certainly was. But I looked at the sight line he made along his index finger and down to the floor. He was pointing. The *zagarettes* were there in the middle of one of the squares, scattered like pick-up sticks, their paper color blended perfectly with the shade of the limestone.

Badi sat next to me on the harbor train, going through my notebooks, looking at the Moghrebi texts I had been working out into what I hoped was a lyrical Russian. The coral trees threw a checkerwork of shadows in through the windows. The dark patterns tumbled over Radetsky's face, sleeping across from us in the breezeless compartment.

Badi said we had been the victim of 'scorpions', or *scorpiones*, hotel con men posing as federal police. We were going over some Dinka songs, and Badi made quick corrections as he spoke. He said we were lucky. Even young *scorpiones* were rumored to be good at set-ups. We had definitely gotten two who were off their game, or, more likely, were themselves too high and disoriented to remember their routine.

Badi came to a song whose final lines I had not yet captured. He tapped his blue pencil on the already smudged, torn paper.

'They grow up in camps, in prisons themselves,' he said. 'They are like the Guardia Civil up in Spain or like Russian police. Good at getting criminals because they have been hoods themselves.'

The lines of the Dinka song had to do with cycles and recurrence. The fronting couplets of the stanza spoke of rains that come, go away, wait in the place they have gone to, and then come again. The winds also come, go away, wait in the place they have gone away to, and then come again. I'd gotten those two lines perfectly.

'They kill,' said Badi. 'Scorpions all lived in the camps of the French, not knowing from one day to the next if they would be around. So they are not afraid. They will make the move without hesitation.'

Badi stopped his tapping.

'What happens to you?' I asked.

'I don't know,' he said, 'but there are places up in the Atlas. Riverbeds, full of bones.'

He changed the words of the final line, which speaks of *[M]an/Who is born, lives, and dies/Goes away to the place he waits in/And does not come back again.*

The cadence was gorgeous, the sounds of the Arabic spectral and cool, like echoes bouncing back across stone. I put my hand on Badi's shoulder and he snapped the notebook shut. Soon he was asleep too.

It would be an hour or two before Tangier, and hours after that waiting for the Algeciras ferry. When I closed my own eyes I saw the two men sitting in the room again. Then I saw lines and lines of the script I was learning, its sharp points and waving upward thrusts, like young grass just starting to come into its growth.

94

Breakthrough

Though the best hunting lands are still mostly west of the Urals, much of its way of life stretches southeast toward the Central Asian steppes. Siberia was and still is a hunter's paradise. The roads toward Ulan-Ude are filled with the brute music of hounds and the knock of guns.

To hunt was to inhabit the land of the dead, Turgenev thought. One's boots drank in the blessedness and silence of Heaven. It was to wander in a place outside of time, and to see in its gray havens sights and portents that lay beyond the understanding of the living.

Odd that the most European and dandified of Russians should love the stalking that was the essential peasant adventure. He dressed 'most fine', the gentle barbarian (Turgenev), but wanted his ankles down in the sheep sorrel, the purple heather and laurel beds and berry-speckled hedgerows. He dined with Flaubert, and always wished to get this master of his out into the 'scrofulous mountains,' the place of the true beasts that stood as the Frenchman's archetypes of hippos, walruses, flightless birds – his famous animal personas. Wretched, hook-nosed ginger horses and *borzoi* dogs walking high off the ground. You still see them here, at home in the limitless yellow and brown, under the limitless blue. Birds come up out of the grass and float in the cross-breezes, their movement no more noticeable than a clock's hands. Turgenev's *Sketches from a Hunter's Album* is an endless fauna catalogue: undergrowth full of robins and siskins and chiffchaffs; finches and white hares racing through mounds of violets and anthills; agaric; fairy clubs and red fly flowers, russela going to crimson from green.

Turgenev would tell Flaubert that the latter's contempt for the bourgeoisie was nonsensical here. This was the sport, *the life*, of emancipation and classlessness, where gentlemen took their servants from farmhouse to farmhouse for days on end. Together they smoked and told stories and bagged Hungarian partridges for their hosts, who fed them like kings and turned over the keys to their *banyas* and larders. Together they slept as youthful brothers in barns fixed up as inns, falling asleep in the hay huddled close as paving stones in the summer dark, watching the coffin-sized barn roof louvers fill with cream-colored stars. Who needed decrees from

Alexander, T. told F., when you lived outside the world that selfdom divided?

On those rare times when Flaubert would come out of his Rouen hermitage and journey down to Turgenev's lodgings at Bougival, the Russian would read passages to the younger man, who could be thunderstruck with admiration:

> One of the principal advantages of hunting,
> dear readers, is that it forces you to travel
> from place to place ... to regimental venues
> like the Lebedyan horse fair.

His story ('Lebedyan') went on and on about the thoroughfares created by lines of carts and crowds of people of every calling, age and appearance:

> [D]ealers in blue caftans and curly-haired gypsies
> with popping eyes, looking horses in the teeth, lifting
> their hooves and tails, shouting, swearing, acting as

go-betweens, making bets or swarming about some remote officer in his army cap and beaver-lined greatcoat. There were Cossacks with their tufts braided and jeweled and peasants in sheepskin jackets torn under the armpits; broad-browed landowners with tinted whiskers and dignified expressions in peakless rectangular caps and camel-cloth jackets worn on one arm only; coachmen in peacock-feathered hats; merchants with short necks and eyes swimming in fat, wheezing their way painfully about.

For all the touted research Flaubert performed for the market scenes of Carthage in *Salammbo*, you cannot help but think their vividness was borrowed wholly from these Russian country sketches, these tapestries of commerce rather than, well, than *hunting*.

But Flaubert would never dream of joining the hunts or hamlet visits himself. To travel this far downriver, to even grant an audience to his greatest of friends – all this was distraction from the real work, which existed alongside that of merely living, and which never touched it. The Master could no more imagine himself hunting than coming down to dinner to discuss the national budget.

An editor I met in Moscow had a great-great-grandfather who worked at Bourgeval. The story he passed down to the editor is, of course, the ultimate Flaubert story, the supreme Turgenev story and the archetypal anecdote of the writer's isolation and accustomed toil. Late in the last century a reporter from *Lundi*, the precursor to *Match*, had been granted access to spend a day with Flaubert in Rouen. The earnest young writer took the night train from the Gare du Nord and was allowed to wash up in the guesthouse, sequestered there all morning while the Master wrote in his fabled cottage.

When the reporter came to the table at lunchtime and Flaubert was shown in, the reporter asked the great man what he had spent the entire morning writing. The Master looked at him and then out at the riverbank. 'I have written,' he said, 'a comma.'

The reporter, crestfallen, went back to the guesthouse and worked up features he was nearing deadline on, his own productivity delighting and giving him hope that something would happen over in the cottage, that his trip would not be in vain.

At dinnertime Flaubert was again shown into the parlor. The reporter brimmed with expectation. The Master stated that he had made a breakthrough. 'A breakthrough,' said the reporter, pulling his pad out and cocking his head. 'Tell me, tell me from what well you have brought it up.'

Flaubert looked down across the table at him, over the scrofulous mountainsides of his moustache, and said: 'I have crossed the comma out.'

95

Time (*Vremya*)

Does the child feel time, or the necessity of filling it? Put another way, does it experience boredom? Does boredom entail discomfort, or can it be mere lassitude, a simple, silent drifting?

How could we determine whether a child (say under six) was bored? To what evidence would we point? It is almost impossible to imagine any kind of proof. At two or three, immobility (or just not moving around that much) and isolation would seem to be indicators. We want to think of a natural curiosity in others, a sociability which, when not demonstrated, demonstrates an aberration.

Where do we draw the line between boredom and complete absence of affect? It is the latter that can be truly noticed (one of the few things that can be) before a child expresses itself in fixed mediums.

When drawing *does* come along, what does the bored child draw? A snow field, reeling 'V's' of birds far off in one corner, maybe a lower corner. Again, we look for an absence of people. (But doesn't the French *ennui* take place in the midst of population, and precisely because of it?)

Boredom, one would think, must involve two concepts utterly strange to a toddler or primary-school child. It would necessitate a sense of time wasted, underutilized, and, conversely, a sense of time stretching out ahead of oneself to a problematic, eventually threatening degree, an unfillable infinity.

To adults, boredom is a treachery of mind, a failure of the means of self-fulfillment. It is not a quality of experience but the absence of quality, the seepage of oblivion into what usually presents itself as thereness.

Some of the primary-schoolers in our unauthorized floor visits stare away into space, away from Barney and out the window. They are not impaired, but nonetheless do nothing with what is put in front of them. They are, the caregivers say, 'not with us today'. They are *away*. *Magda is away.*

Still, we cannot imagine it (boredom) in them. We want to see it as something else, perhaps distraction. (And how different from *ennui* is that? It is still a chasing after substance.)

We want the most pernicious of afflictions to be had

only by the potentially pernicious minds, the adults'. To imagine it any other way is to imagine the evaporation of childhood, or at least a diminishment of its lines of demarcation. Larkin talked of older children, and then of people older than that (when does childhood end?). He spoke of these stages only when he wrote:

Life is first boredom, then fear
Whether or not we use it, it goes.
And leaves what something hidden from us chose,
And age, and then the only end of age.

96

Time (*Vremya*) II

The fragmentation of consciousness, its piecemeal nature so obvious in the orphans from a first glance. It is all congealing, blasting apart, congealing a little more the next time with a kind of tighter gravity, so the fragmentation is slower, harder, releasing more power. Their first experience of self is that it is multitudinous. And where else do the greatest artists end up with it? Whitman ('I contain multitudes') and Proust: how much of one's multitudinous self can a person embody at once? How long before the next blast into fragments and the next gathering in?

No matter how we proceed, no matter how we go about it, we cannot be all of ourselves at once. The infant begins what we all end up doing: living by synecdoche and by vivid fragments of being. Their clarity can be faint or tremendous. They build upon each other, overlapping like shingles that eventually smooth themselves and blend in color. Personality consists of fluctuations followed by steadiness, a visionary goo wobbling on a pivot, and the pivot holding.

Again, watching the babies readied for bed, one sees the hint of Proust's first memory of betrayal. For him, a child of wealth, the refusal of his mother's goodnight kiss at the beginning of the *Search* begins it all, the heightening ladder of disappointment. The little boy gets the kiss, and revels in the power and freedom he finds when triumphing over his mother's refusal to leave her guests and come to his room to deliver the *besse*. But as soon as he scores this victory, his parents' capitulation bestows an aftertaste of disappointment. He loses a bit of the willpower to control his moods when one wish gets satisfied. He has to plot the next entreaty, the next respondent, whether or not he really wants his desire satisfied.

But Proust family albums show simpler dynamics in answers he wrote to basic questions about attachment and estrangement. *What is for you the greatest unhappiness?* To be separated from Maman; not to have known my mother and grandmother. *In what place would you like to live?* In the land of the Ideal, or rather of my ideal. In the place where certain things I want would come to pass as if by enchantment – and where tender feelings would always be shared.

Enchantment this early in life stays at the door of the great blue communal bedroom. It stays on the lacquer bowls of visiting firebirds and angel-souled speaking pike. All cry out when the door is closed and no one comes back until morning. To cry, to wonder what crying will bring, is to work a lever that may be connected to nothing.

Until the baby reaches a wider wisdom, all that is about her is overwhelming and only occasionally controllable. The best she can hope for for now, the only structure the multitudes can have, is to lean themselves on someone's love.

97

Last Nights

We plop Amelia in her hated snowsuit and trudge through the good blocks of Tsverskaya: by the Ryabushinsky House, the Korsh Theater and Gubin Estate. The great boulevard sparkles with lighted snowdrifts, fading and brightening in the wind. Minstrels' notes come up from the street underpasses and Metro entrances. I will use one of these vast culverts for two more days to get diapers, mashed vegetables, Ukrainian wheat vodka with grass blades suspended in the amber litre.

An old apartment house contains in its alley a new Adriatic restaurant run and peopled by Italian expats. But the waiters are Russian and frustrated by my cumbersome ordering. They stand in the corners, talking among themselves, turning to glare at my wife's unpacking of her diaper bag, the baby's kicking and crying. We leave early.

I wash down a sleeping pill with Imperia vodka and fear bad dreams. I am not disappointed.

It is the dream of the nation of waiters, of the nervous waiters. I had it first in Bahia on our honeymoon. Immaculate men with especially bright eyes, ethnically indistinguishable, come to the table with a plate of odd shrimp that seems slightly alive. You figure simply that you have been drinking. You've been drinking at home just to work up the time and the courage to come.

The creatures on the plate are waxen and gray. They hum with the kind of electrical buzz that animated a lot of the scenes of *Eraserhead*. When you shove back the plate, brown puddles of sauce make a trail on the cloth.

You are asked if you want a new course. You assent with a bow and they bow back. Your teeth feel suddenly heavy, like pebbles. You imagine them dropping through your body as through a tank of water, as if being toothless would solve the problem.

The next course they bring is a ghost of the first: wet, softening shells that curl and then dry before your eyes. They blow away like leaves across the open patio.

Then there is a last course, one that you have only the vaguest anticipation of yet which causes you great sorrow and sympathy for them. All your instruments of empathy are at full tilt. You brim with the apologies of your race and class.

More men are behind the men that waited on you.

They signal to you with their large knives to walk out with them to the hill. They remind you to bring the soup spoon. You bend down, without asking, and dig. You dig the shape of yourself in the ground, two feet, perhaps three feet deep. They lean down to cut and to fold you, still slightly alive, into the hole.

98

Sunbeam

Pity the poor holy man, pity his going up and his coming back. No one wants to listen to sermons, especially children. They do not even want to listen to songs.

But they can especially see through their caregivers being forced to sing along with the Orthodox Patriarchs who come into the schools now on holidays. The Patriarchs tell Bible stories: Bathsheba and David, David and Goliath, Nebuchadnezzar fumbling with his gold staff through the clover. (The prideful, still the West, capitalism, being brought low.)

But the caregivers, whether sixty or twenty, are Soviets down to the last corpuscle, materialists to the last atom. The ones who are twenty have mothers who were Young Pioneers, so the atheistic given is not yet washed out, and may never be. It is not that life is incomprehensible and unendurable without God, but that God is not the opiate to get you through the incomprehensible and unendurable.

It is not so much that those who care for these children don't see some usefulness in the Church. As with generations even under the sickle and star, the Church was a cultural (old culture) unifier, and the source/receptacle of superstition and luck. To pray to the icon wasn't so much to seek guidance on where to go and what to do, how to conduct one's life, as it was to get an amulet for what had already been done. You prayed to the Virgin of Novgorod not so much to find out where to walk, how to step, what to lie down upon. You prayed that where you walked and rested left nothing sticking to you.

The Patriarch is sitting in the corner. The thirtyish caregivers sing an old Kiev hymn. They stare straight ahead and swallow. They are like pilots trying to use bad weather for extra lift. They put their heads down, hands to the throttle, and sing to the God they were raised to ignore.

99

Yaroslavl

Many children from the orphanages leave with no sense of geography, at the most very little. One thinks of G.E. Moore's old axioms in 'Proof Of An External World.' You know two things. One is that the hand you hold up in front of your face is your own. The other is that you have never been more than five, six, eight miles from the surface of the earth.

My friend's two girls (siblings, seven and five) knew nothing but the orphanage from their earliest memory. Their children's home was in an old Soviet naval base on the Volga. They had only been outside its walls to see the river: the silver monolith, its waves at once unmoving and overlapping, silently falling into themselves.

Maps and what they represented were simply another thing they ignored in pre-school and primary school and from the intermittent imploring of adults. Yaroslavl, with its church of sixteen steeples, Yaroslavl the ancient kingdom seat that steadied the culture, the language they cleave to now so zealously in the States – they knew it only barely and only as the outer extremity of the earth.

They still think, living in Northern California, that they are in some appendage or peninsula of the Russian nation. They speak to each other of swimming in the Volga again this coming summer, and have a notion that the many bridges and barges they see from their parents' windows prove them to be not far from where they started out. They point to the ocean, remembering that someone told them there were places the Volga was so wide you could not see to the other side of it.

Some nights, my friend and his wife spread the atlas out and explain the distances. But like the Kara-Khaaks of Tuva, the girls see cartography as shaping only a place that immediately surrounds them. All maps are local. There is nothing in the colored land and water bodies, which they sometimes mix up, to indicate that days of travel are entailed between them.

Sometimes their father takes them to the top of Coit Tower. He gets them to remember the plane ride, knowing that they watched themselves cross Greenland, and that this took time – the time between lunch and when they had to go to the bathroom after lunch. As the sky darkened outside the plane windows, he thought he saw something registering in their eyes as they watched the same yellow clusters – towns of Acadia and Manitoba – cross from one end of the porthole to the other, or to the window behind them in that empty row of seats they ran to. He points to the farthest shores of Marin, and lets them lean against him in the same way they did, with the same pull and drift of the plane banking, when they first looked down on the lights of earth.

100

Measuring Space

I walked out onto the back porch of the orphanage, wondering how I'd begin the adoption book: whether to let it grow out of this one, start something afresh, a hybrid of the two, etcetera. I could hear the dinnertime singing of the children from the third-story window. I took a Ukrainian newspaper out of the trash can so I could sit down on the icy steps. Through the bottom of my ski pants I could feel sharp chunks of sprinkled cinders sticking up through the spread newsprint.

I slowly peeled the orange I'd brought with me, trying to separate and spread the skin in the manner of the earliest map-makers. I ripped it on the third try. The singing rose and smoothed its harmonies as I picked the segments apart, wondering whether this was the orange I'd injected with the syringe of vodka.

Getting a baby, starting a story, I realized, was all part of the same grab at eternity your life so far had always told you shouldn't even think of trying. These acts of creation were not additional facts of existence, but were more like an unshifting frame that held all other facts together – a measuring space that made them exist or not exist, or at least made them true or false (not the same thing).

Fifty, though, was a formidable age to be taking these things on. I looked down at my old, familiar body, regarding it as carefully, with the same fondness and doubt, as I would have if it were stretched out on a hammock in the tropics. I had spread the paper as much out of fear of losing my footing as from wanting to avoid the feel of the cinders. I knew elderly caretakers had slipped on icy steps, and toddlers. It struck me suddenly that I was coming into the company of the former. Never in my life had I worried about falling on ice. But now I was as likely to do it as an old man or someone who had only begun to walk.

I looked up at the cloudlets, the puffs of smeltworks smoke, whatever they were, in the violet sky. My eyes searched the birch and cork grove for another soul, something else, as I popped the first orange segments into my mouth. No vodka. But the taste of all of the south in which the fruit had grown. A little orb of Tunis or of Malta.

The childrens' voices became majestic, though the song was just a railroad or timber camp anthem, possibly an old marching song of the Young Pioneers. Having never had a claim on anyone's affections, they were building for themselves the next best thing: a present afterlife, a paradise of happiness they could inhabit in the radiant, continuous chain of framing spaces their singing made. My poet friend had written that '[I]t is the ordinary that is the miracle', and had followed it with two couplets:

> Ordinary love and ordinary death,
> ordinary suffering, ordinary birth

> the ordinary couplets of our breath,
> ordinary heaven, ordinary earth

The voices became sweeter and sweeter. They were like the twees and whistles of nightingales through the winter orchard, a deep hymn of need and of love. This was the companion-call of the human, the heart of the heart of the human. Its cadences and pauses smelled like birch and cork wood, and tasted of oranges.

Source Notes for Postcards

15 Elias Canetti, *Crowds and Power*; 22 Fyodor Dostoevsky, *A Writer's Diary* and Joseph Frank, *Dostoevsky: The Stir of Liberatio*; 23&24 Radzinsky, *The Rasputin File*; 26 Paustovsky, *The Golden Rose*; 28&33 Constance Garnett trans.; 32&40 James Forsyth, *A History of the Peoples of Siberia*; 41 Alexander Herzen, *Out of My Past and Thoughts*, Garnett & MacDonald trans.; 43 Mircea Eliade, *Shamanism: Archaic Techniques of Ecstasy* and Piers Vitebsky, *The Shaman: Voyages of the Soul*; 48 Joseph Frank, *Dostoevsky: The Miraculous Years*; 54 Nadezhda Mandelstam, *Hope Against Hope* and *Hope Abandoned*; 55 Alexander Solzhenitsyn, *The Gulag Archipelago*; 57 *Gulag: A Pictorial History of The Soviet Concentration Camps*; 58 Colin Thubron, *In Siberia*; 74 Waldemar Bogoras, *The Chuckchee and Chuckchee Mythology*; 76 George Kennan, *Siberia and the Exile System*; 91 'Tyumen' is an adaptation, into a West Siberian context, of David Malouf's story 'Closer', in *Dream Stuff*. Grateful acknowledgment is made to Mr. Malouf and his agent, Deborah Rogers; 100 Derek Walcott, *Tiepolo's Hound*.